comin
2gt u

Simon Packham was born in Brighton. During his time as an actor he was a blind fiddler on HMS Bounty, a murderous vicar, a dodgy witness on The Bill and a variety of servants including Omar Sharif's personal footman and a coffin carrier for Dame Judi Dench. He now writes fiction and lives in West Sussex with his wife, two children, a cat called Pax, and a variety of hamsters.

comin 2 gt u

SIMON PACKHAM

PICCADILLY PRESS • LONDON

For Mum and Dad

First published in Great Britain in 2010
by Piccadilly Press Ltd,
5 Castle Road, London NW1 8PR
www.piccadillypress.co.uk

Text copyright © Simon Packham, 2010

A catalogue record for this book is available
from the British Library

ISBN: 978 1 84812 095 2 (paperback)

1 3 5 7 9 10 8 6 4 2

Printed in the UK by CPI Bookmarque, Croydon, CR0 4TD
Cover design and photo by Patrick Knowles

THURSDAY
(WEEK ONE)

9.05 p.m.

I'd only been in World 67 two hours when I realised they were going to murder me. A mini movie of my whole life flickered through my head and I cursed myself for letting them lead me into such a barren hellhole.

Letz go bak, I pleaded, knowing from their silence that Duke77 (aka me, Sam Tennant) would soon be history.

But don't go thinking I was some kind of fresh-faced noob. I'd been working for weeks to get my levels up. I should have spotted a couple of scammers a mile off. So why had I wandered into the wilderness with two complete strangers? I was about to start begging when the conversation turned nasty:

Ollyg78: U r so dead

The Emperor: Dont kill him yet i wanna du it
Ollyg78: Kk

Beads of perspiration trickled down my torso as we circumnavigated the yellow lakes of molten lava and picked our way through a forest of dying trees, their branches gnarled and twisted, like Granddad's arthritic fingers.

Duke 77: Plz . . . ill give you my amulet of glory . . . fully charged
The Emperor: Lol chickenboy
Ollyg78: Noob head
Duke77: Y u doing this
Ollyg78: Der thats really bait
The Emperor: Coz wi hate you.

It was all over in a nanosecond. I'd never died before, but like Alex said, the graphics were really primitive. The Emperor slashed at me with his dragon scimitar and there were a few random splats of blood before I sank to my knees and snuffed it.

But it was what came next that really threw me.

Ollyg78: g2g cya l8r sam
The Emperor: C ya tomorrow in pshe

They knew who I was.
But that was impossible. How could they? If they'd been

in my tutor group, I would have recognised their profiles.

The Emperor: Well be watching u
Ollyg78: We know whr you live
The Emperor: Were comin 2 gt u
Duke77: Who r u wat u want
Unable to send message, player has logged out.

And when I respawned, I'd lost everything – all the cool stuff I'd worked so hard for: full dragon, my amulet of glory (fully charged), a million lobsters, a hundred cut diamonds, five thousand castle wars tokens, ten thousand flax and, worst of all, my elf crystal armour. I felt like someone had just taken my whole life and flushed it down the lavatory.

'Samuel! It's time you were off that computer.'

If I'd had a pound for every time Mum stood at the bottom of the stairs and shouted that, I wouldn't have needed to waste valuable gaming hours cleaning out those stinking chickens to pay her back for my iPod Nano.

'Yeah, all right, I was just logging off anyway.'

'Well hurry up then. No wonder you never have any time for your clarinet practice.'

According to Mum, I spent half my life on the internet and the other half 'brushing up my serial killing skills' on the Xbox. Can *you* see a problem with that?

'Come on, Sam. You should have been in bed twenty minutes ago.'

She'd been loads stricter these past few weeks since Dad flew off to the States to 'follow his dream'. It's always been quite relaxed in our house, but it was getting more like being in the army every day. If I turned up like two seconds late for tea or something, Mum went ballistic.

'Can I just —'

'No, you can't. I've hardly seen you since I got home. You haven't told me about school yet.'

She had this wacko idea that parents ought to know everything about their kids' lives. Just because she was a child psychiatrist she thought she was an expert on children. And she kept telling me I should try to be more interested in other people. So I went downstairs to work on my social skills. 'Hi Mum, how was your day?'

'Oh, the usual: a suspected Asperger's and a couple of ADHDs.' Now that she'd got me there she seemed more interested in the TV. 'But what about you, Sam; you look a bit down in the dumps, is everything all right?'

'Something really weird just happened.'

'What do you mean weird? You've not been in those chat rooms, have you?'

Every time I went online she gave me the big speech about not revealing my name and address.

'No, Mum, nothing like that – someone just killed me.'

'I thought that was the whole point.'

'Yes but —'

'It's only a game, Sam. I wish you took the rest of your life so seriously. Now come on, what happened at school?'

Personally, I think that sort of information should be on a need-to-know basis, but I knew that I if didn't spill a few random beans about St Thomas's Community College she'd wear me down like one of those poor kids she called her clients.

'Alex has got this brilliant new MP4 player.'

'Lucky old Alex.'

'Callum Corcoran and his mate Animal put opened sachets of mayonnaise on the steps of the modern languages block.'

'Callum's the child with the anger management issues, right?'

'You could say that.' Although total psychopath would have been nearer the mark.

'What about lessons?'

'We did global warming again. I told them all that funny stuff you said about dumb blondes with scary nail extensions who do the school-run in their four-by-fours. Even Miss Stanley was smiling.'

'I hope you're not becoming the class clown, Samuel.'

'I'm working on it. Which reminds me, "I'll do the funnies" wants the *HMS Belfast* money by Monday morning or we can't go.'

Mum gave me the look she usually reserved for Dad's DIY. 'It's been on the piano since last week. Put it in your rucksack now so you don't forget.'

'Cool.'

She squeezed me tightly and planted her lips on the back of my head. Maybe I was getting too old for good-night kisses, but I really liked the smell of her perfume.

'Night night, love. You will remember to clean your teeth, won't you? Your breath's a bit . . .'

'Yes, Mum.'

'And it might be a good time to call your dad. You know how much he likes to hear from you. Why do you think he got you that phone?'

'Night, Mum.'

'Love you.'

And *I* loved *her*, more than anything in the world, but like Dad said, it didn't mean I had to say so every five seconds. 'Me too,' I grunted, and headed for the stairs. 'Oh . . . Mum?'

'What is it now?' she said, zapping a desperate house-wife with the remote. 'You haven't forgotten your food tech ingredients, have you?'

'No, it's not that, it's Granddad.'

'I see.'

I'd taken to visiting Granddad virtually every day. Dad wanted me to keep an eye on him while he was in the States, and Mum didn't like me coming home to an empty house. He was good company too – even if he was 'pushing ninety'.

'How is the old devil anyway?'

'He's says he's got this massive secret. The only trouble is he doesn't know how to tell me yet.'

'Sounds just like Ray. He always knew how to spin out a yarn. Send him my love when you see him tomorrow.'

Mum often sent Granddad her love, but she never brought it in person. 'Yeah . . . OK. Night, Mum.'

'And make sure you don't fall asleep with your earphones in.'

Even I had to admit, it was a total beast: 3.2 megapixel

camera, video-messaging, Bluetooth and an awesome, sliding keypad. I should have realised there wos a catch when he gave it to me. 'I'll keep it topped up for you,' he said. 'Then you can get in contact whenever you need me. We could call it the "Dad Phone" if you want . . . you know, like the "Bat Phone"?'

And then he told me he was running away to join the Hardmen. 'It's something I've always dreamed about. Working from home is convenient of course, but I've never been terribly interested in IT support, Sam. So your mother and I have decided that I'm going to take six weeks' unpaid leave to try my luck on the world veterans' tour. If I don't do it now, I never will.'

It had all started with the London Marathon. Mum had persuaded him to run it with a wind turbine on his head and, from that moment, Dad was hooked. At weekends he used to drag us off to Luton or Leicester or somewhere and we'd stand in the pouring rain whilst he plodded twenty-six miles in just over four hours. But after a while, mere marathons weren't enough for him. He graduated to triathlons, then quadrathons, and just when we thought it couldn't get any worse, he discovered the Hardman Circuit. 'The rest's mere child's play,' he said. 'If a man really wants to test himself, a five kilometre swim, two hundred and twelve kilometre bike ride, forty-eight-hour hike in full body armour, followed by a double marathon is the only way to do it.'

Mum said it was better than dyeing his hair and running off with the woman on the Sainsbury's cheese counter. But at least kids whose parents were divorced got to hook up with their dads in Pizza Express every other Saturday. And Alex's mum had just bought him a proper DJ's mixing desk – not that he'd ever use it of course.

I was supposed to call Dad every day. The funny thing was, now that he wasn't living with us, I could never think of anything to say.

'Hi, Dad.'

'Hi, Sam,' he yawned. 'What news?'

'Nothing much.'

'Good, good . . . that's . . . good.'

'How's the training going?'

'Yeah, yeah, fine. I jogged ten kilometres this morning just to keep loose, but I'm trying to have a power nap.'

'Been up the Empire State Building yet?'

'You must be joking. I'm not here to enjoy myself.'

'No . . . course not.'

'What about you, Sam? Still sticking to that schedule I gave you?'

Dad thought I was training for a Junior Hardman event in Milton Keynes. I hadn't the heart to tell him I'd rather push a ping pong ball up the M1 with my nose.

'Yes, Dad.'

'Good lad. Find out what you're really passionate about and hang on to it for dear life. That's the best advice anyone's ever given me.'

'I saw Granddad today.'

I knew he still felt guilty about him, I could tell from his voice. 'Is he any happier do you think? Did he get that CD I sent him? Is he eating properly?'

'Last week he asked me to take him some fish and chips.'

'Well, that's a relief. Your granddad always loved his food.'

'But you should hear some of the stuff he comes out with. Why don't you talk to him, Dad?'

'He knows my number. I gave him a phone just like yours.'

'He can't even switch it on.'

'Yes, well . . . I'm sure he could work it out if he wanted to.'

'Yeah but —'

'How's Mum? Still crusading for the council to start recycling tetra packs? Send her my love won't you?'

'I could go and get her if you —'

'No, it's OK; I spoke to her earlier . . . Bye, Sam.'

I always wanted to tell him how much we both missed him, how life just wasn't the same without someone to watch *Top Gear* and do Homer impressions with. But Dad was a Hardman now; he didn't want me behaving like a little kid. He just wanted me to get on with it.

'Night night, Dad.'

There was something else I couldn't tell Dad. He'd have laughed his head off if I'd told him about my *real* passion. It wasn't my slick new iPod Nano – although Mum said if the house was on fire I'd leave her to burn and save the iPod first – and it wasn't Ben & Jerry's Chunky Monkey. No, my real passion, and my *numero uno* bedtime listening, was the one and only Mr Duke

9

Ellington. Not that I'd have gone blabbing to the likes of Callum Corcoran about my obsession with 1930s' jazz; he was more of a R 'n' B man, and practically the whole of Year Eight witnessed Corky's way of settling an artistic dispute that time Ben W suggested *Spider-Man 2* was better than the first.

But I almost wished Corky could bipod with me right now, because I actually thought he'd love it if he gave it a chance. I knew he would.

And Granddad was right; the early stuff is the best. Jungle music they called it; the hot sounds of the Cotton Club, with Duke at the piano and the great Bubber Miley growling away on trumpet. Granddad described it as 'three minutes of unadulterated musical bliss'. I'm still not sure what he meant by that, but whenever I heard 'Rockin' in Rhythm', I couldn't help getting this great big grin on my face.

Except that night, it wasn't happening. Every time my mouth tried to twist upwards into a smile, I got this terrible feeling that something wasn't quite right. I kept going over the gory details of my recent death and every time I closed my eyes, I saw a dragon scimitar hovering above my head.

I checked my lesson planner, trying to convince myself it was just a couple of random kids having a laugh. The two-weekly timetable was always a bit confusing, but I was pretty certain we were coming to the end of week one, which meant that I *did* have PSHE second lesson on Friday morning. It could have been a lucky guess, right? Then again, what if The Emperor and Ollyg78 really did know me? Who were they? And why did they seem to hate me so much?

I peered into the deserted street, scanning the wheelie bins for hidden assassins, checking the bus shelter for spies. Mum was always saying I had an overactive imagination, but I couldn't help wondering if they were out there watching me.

FRIDAY
(WEEK ONE)

8.30 a.m.

When I started at St Thomas's, Mum insisted on dropping me at the main gate. By the summer term of Year Eight, I'd finally persuaded her it would make the journey to work much easier if I slipped out at the bottom of the hill.

'Bye love. Hope your shortbread turns out all right.'

'Bye Mum; good luck with your school phobic.' And before she had time to lean across the gearstick and kiss me, I'd dived onto the pavement and joined the straggly line of blue sweatshirts lugging twice their body weight up to school in their customised rucksacks.

I'd calmed down a bit since the night before. I figured I might not be as popular as Gaz Lulham or Pete Hughes, but at least the other kids always laughed at my silly jokes.

It was hard to believe that anyone in Year Eight actually hated me.

Even so, I was pleased when I spotted the hunched figure of my best friend, dawdling along in front of me – mobile in one hand, his new electric guitar in the other.

'Oi . . . Lex . . . Wait up!'

I'd known Alex, like forever. We'd hung out in the sand-pit together at nursery, and our parents had been barbecue buddies until Mr Pitts had discovered Facebook.

'Yo, Lex, why weren't you online last night?'

'Dad took us to meet his new girlfriend.'

'What's she like then?'

'Better than the last one; at least she didn't try to be our friend.'

'Any kids?'

He stared gloomily into his mobile. 'Two girls.'

No wonder he looked depressed. 'Sorry about that.'

'Molly loved it. The little one was about the same age as her. They spent the whole time dressing up stupid rodent things and pushing them about in a plastic boat.'

'What about the other one?'

Lex stopped texting for a moment. 'She was all right, I suppose.' But I knew he was putting a brave face on it; his ears always went red when he was upset about something.

'So, what did you do all night?'

'You don't want to know.'

'That bad, huh?'

He nodded grimly. I had a chilling vision of poor Lex struggling to stay awake in front of the latest *Sims (Pets)* or prancing about to SingStar. 'Don't worry; your dad'll probably have found another new Facebook friend by next week.'

'Ha . . . ha.'

Unfortunately, Alex didn't have much sense of humour where his dad's 'lady friends' were concerned.

'Hey, Lex – did you know that diarrhoea is hereditary.'

'What?'

'Yeah – it runs in your jeans!'

Not a flicker. Things must have been worse than I thought; he didn't look up from his texting the whole way to the main gate. Mobiles and MP3 players were strictly forbidden, so there was always a bottleneck while everyone set their phones to vibrate and stuffed them into their pockets.

'Don't you get it? It runs in your jeans.'

It was the next bit I hated most: the mad stampede through the gates, the random kicking, the older kids swearing at you and a lump in your throat the size of a tennis ball. I don't mind admitting that for the first couple of terms I was a whistle away from doing the one thing that Dad had warned me about. 'For God's sake, don't cry,' he'd said, as he'd snapped yet another photo of me in my new uniform. 'One boy at my school cried on his first day, and they were still calling him "the boy who cried" on the last day of the Sixth Form.'

Now I was in Year Eight I could handle it. I didn't even get that shivery feeling when the crowd thinned out and I got my first proper view of the maths suite. Dad said St Thomas's reminded him of a state-of-the-art prison, but as long as you kept your head down, it wasn't that bad.

'Oh look,' bellowed a familiar voice. 'It's Noddy and Big Ears.'

Callum Corcoran and his sidekick, Animal, appeared outside the ICT suite, rucksacks whistling around their heads like helicopter blades. I tried to look unconcerned, but Alex's ears had already started transforming.

'Sorry, mate,' said Animal, as his rucksack made contact with Alex's head, 'didn't see you there.'

Callum Corcoran brayed like a demented donkey. 'What, with those lugholes? You blind or something?'

'Hey guys,' I said, spotting the fear in Alex's eyes despite the new designer frames, 'got a joke for you.'

'Oh yeah, what's that then?' said Callum, sounding about as enthusiastic as Simon Cowell.

So I told him. And fortunately he found it a lot funnier than Alex. Animal cracked up the moment he heard the word diarrhoea, and Callum waved his hand in the air like a rapper. 'Oi, Gazzer, you gotta hear this.'

My best friend's ears were slowly returning to normal. 'You all right, Lex?'

'Why shouldn't I be?'

'You look a bit . . . I don't know.'

'Well, I'm not, OK?' He pushed his glasses back up his nose and walked slowly towards main reception.

'Where are you going?'

'Got to take my guitar to the music department.' He

turned to face me as the reception doors slid open in front of him. 'Sam . . . ?'

'Yes.' It was almost like he wanted to tell me something.

'. . . Nothing.'

'What's up? Is something the . . . ' But the automatic doors had already swallowed him alive. Poor old Lex, he'd not been himself for a while. Mum said lots of children found it difficult to adjust to new domestic circumstances. I'd just have to think of a clever new way to cheer him up.

But that would have to wait. The nagging thought I'd succeeded in silencing for a couple of hours had forced its way into my head again, and it was begging for attention. There were only seventy-five minutes until PSHE. What if my internet murderers were about to introduce themselves? What if they were coming to get me?

9.55 a.m.

I glanced back at the rest of the class, half expecting something weird to happen, but no one gave me the evils and as soon as Mr Catchpole started fiddling with the interactive whiteboard I had the feeling that everything was going to be all right.

'Like your jacket, Sir. Did you get it from the Cancer shop?'

'Yes, thank you, Chelsea. I'll do the funnies.'

A huge cheer went up for Catchpole's catchphrase.

'Now hurry up and hand out those worksheets. I want to get on.'

'What we doing, Sir?' said Callum Corcoran, screwing up a worksheet and chucking it at Alex. 'Not puberty again?'

Animal cracked up at the mere mention of the word puberty.

'Not global warming?' said Chelsea. 'I hate global warming.'

'That's the whole point,' said Pete Hughes, running a hand through his carefully gelled hair.

Mr Catchpole hammered on his desk. 'Look, can we have a bit of hush please? Now before we start, who's remembered their *HMS Belfast* money?'

I was the only one with my hand up.

'Anyone would think you lot didn't want to go.'

'I'm really looking forward to it, Sir,' I said, foraging around in my rucksack for the envelope. 'My granddad was in the navy. He's got a war wound and everything.'

'Thank you for that charming snippet of family history, Samuel, but I'm trying to teach here.'

'Don't worry, sir,' sniggered Callum Corcoran. 'You'll learn how to do it properly in the end.'

'Right, now this is what I want to happen. First of all, I'm going to talk through the worksheets and then we'll do a role-playing exercise,' (chorus of groans) 'before finishing up with a couple of videos.' (Ironic cheers.) 'So, who can tell me what bullying is? *Anyone?* All right, Tristram, we'll start with you.'

Animal put his little finger up to his mouth, like Doctor Evil. 'It's when some kid really gets on your nerves and you, sort of like, accidentally, blap him a bit too hard.'

17

'Yes, well, I'm glad you lot think that's funny, because bullying is actually a very serious issue.'

'I thought *you* were the only one who did the funnies, Mr Catchpole,' came a voice from the back.

'OK, someone else. Yes, you.'

He obviously didn't know her name, which was hardly surprising because no one had heard Abby say more than a couple of sentences all year. She spent most of the time reading or practising her clarinet. I only knew her because she sat next to me in wind band. I'd tried to make her laugh once, by saying she reminded me of one of those nuns who'd sworn a vow of silence, but she'd looked at me like I was mad or something.

'Come on, come on, we haven't got all day.'

A blush spread across Abby's face, like a map of Russia. She folded her arms tightly across her chest and stared down at the table top. 'It's when someone . . .'

'Speak up, for heaven's sake. This is a classroom, not the whispering gallery.'

The Russian Empire extended further down her neck.

'It's when someone wants to have power over somebody else, and they'll do almost anything to get it.'

Mr Catchpole nodded grudgingly. 'As a working definition that's not at all bad. So, bullying.' He scrawled the word on the interactive whiteboard. 'When *I* was at school it was often of a question of intimidation – stealing another pupil's dinner money, that kind of thing. But that's all changed now . . .'

'We don't have dinner money no more,' said Chelsea.

'We have them swipe cards.'

'And Queen Victoria's dead, Sir.'

'Yes, thank you, Callum. I'll do the funnies.'

Another cheer went up.

'Twenty-first-century bullying is a very different kettle of fish. Let's start with the internet . . .'

Mr Catchpole took us through a long list of bullying techniques, some of which I'm sure Callum Corcoran hadn't even thought of yet. Despite his catchphrase, old Catchpole was a really boring speaker (in fact, I couldn't remember him *ever* saying anything funny) and I soon found myself daydreaming about Granddad's big secret; kind of wondering if he was going to leave me some money or a share in a race-horse or something.

'. . . it could be that you speak differently, or the colour of your skin . . .'

And anyway, now that I was fairly confident The Emperor business was just a random wind-up, I didn't think I had much to worry about. Catchpole's catalogue of potential victims didn't include anyone like me. Sadly for Alex, he seemed to fit the bill on a couple of counts (smaller than average, wore glasses). Maybe it was just as well he'd gone for his guitar lesson.

'OK, when you've written up the notes, we'll start on some role-play.'

Abby looked none too thrilled to be the victim, blinking rapidly and winding a strand of her fine, mousey hair around an index finger. Callum on the other hand was really getting into the part of the bully. He circled his prey like a professional, bursting into song in his peculiarly deep, yet occasionally squeaky, voice: '*I wore my brace of many colours, ooo.*'

I was supposed to be the 'bystander'. I'd even been given my own catchphrase: 'Don't just stand by, stand by me.' Only I didn't have a clue how to go about it, so I stood there like a lemon, with a stupid grin on my face.

'. . . and you're a real porker,' continued Callum. 'Did you know that, A–BIG–gail? Ha, ha, ha, ha . . .'

That was the moment when Abby should have said thank you and walked away, or confronted her persecutor with an assertive (but not aggressive) 'No'. Unfortunately, she just turned a deeper shade of red.

'And her mum's a right slapper,' chipped in Chelsea.

Abby was fighting back the tears. I knew that's what she was doing because biting hard on my bottom lip was the only thing that had stopped me crying when I kept getting lost in the first term. If I didn't do something soon, there'd be tears before lunchtime.

'Hey, Corky,' I shouted. 'Why did the toilet roll roll down the hill?'

Callum stared at me like a cat that had suddenly got two mice to choose from. The whole room went silent (apart from Animal, who started sniggering as soon as he heard the word toilet) and I wished I'd kept my big mouth shut. 'Why did the *wot*?'

'Er . . . why did the toilet roll roll down the hill?' Callum flexed his knuckles and I hit him with the punchline. 'To get to the bottom!'

I held my breath, hoping against hope that Callum hadn't lost his passion for toilet humour. At the first burst of his machine-gun laughter – 'Ha, ha, ha, ha, ha, ha, ha,' – I realised I was going to live to fight another day.

Pretty soon the whole class was laughing with him – everyone except Abby, who crept, gratefully, back to her place, and an almost equally red-faced Mr Catchpole. 'Quiet . . . quiet, the lot of you. I've had just about enough of your tomfoolery for one morning. And as for you, Samuel Tennant, I thought I'd made it perfectly clear that I'll do the . . .'

And we all joined in with his catchphrase.

The videos were well boring. First up was a load of celebrities talking about how they'd got picked on at school, followed by a badly-acted, low-budget affair about a boy called Albert who gets bullied because he's rubbish at football. I was about to die of terminal boredom when I felt my phone vibrating. It must have been Alex texting me from his guitar lesson – probably to apologise for being so touchy that morning.

Mr Catchpole sat engrossed, as if *Bertie's Bad Day* was an Oscar-winning blockbuster or something. I reached surreptitiously into my back pocket, concealing my mobile beneath the table while I checked it out. The message was short and sweet, but it wasn't from Alex.

Prepare 2 meet ur doom

10.55 a.m.

'What's the matter,' said Alex, 'something wrong with it?'

'Eh?'

'Your cheese and tomato panini; I thought you liked those things?'

'Not hungry,' I said, casting a wary eye around the canteen, wondering if the person who'd sent me that text was wolfing down a carton of spicy sausage pasta and having a good old laugh at me. We normally ate lunch at first break, otherwise I'd have been starving by second break at one thirty. That morning, I didn't feel much like food at all. 'You can have it if you want.'

'No thanks, got to go in a minute.'

'You haven't, have you?'

Alex smiled and slung his new Reebok rucksack over his shoulder. 'Chess club, I always go to chess club first break on Fridays.'

'Oh yeah . . . course.'

'What's the matter, Sam? You OK?'

I wanted to tell him, I really did, but Dad said you should never let on if you're scared; it makes you look weak. And anyway, what was there to be scared of? It was pretty obvious that my doom-mongering text messager was just someone from PSHE experimenting with his new bullying techniques. At least, that's what I kept telling myself. After, all, I'd made it through to lunch without coming to a sticky end, hadn't I?

All the same, I didn't want Alex to go just yet. So, even though I can't stand football, I tried to get him started on his favourite subject: 'How did Man U get on?'

'Real supporters never call us Man U. We're United, or The Reds, but never Man U, OK?'

'Sorry I spoke.'

Alex squinted nervously at the spiky-haired Year Nines hanging out by the drinks machine. 'Look, I've got to go, OK – see you later.'

I normally spent the rest of first break wandering randomly round the courtyard, listening to the latest *Doctor Who* debate or maybe joining in a game of Manhunt. But that morning, I just wasn't up for it. Maybe there really was someone out there who hated me. Maybe, just maybe, it was Ollyg78 or The Emperor who'd sent me that text.

I lingered over my lukewarm panini, trying to convince myself that I was being stupid. But I couldn't help thinking about what Granddad said when they'd told him he'd be better off in a retirement home: 'Just because you're paranoid, doesn't mean to say that no one's out to get you.'

'*Ouch!* What was . . . ?'

I'm not sure what came first, the stinging blow to my forehead or the raucous cheer. All I remember is the gross sensation of something warm and sticky, trickling slowly down my left cheek. Suddenly I saw red. And . . . 'Oh my God, I'm bleeding!'

I rifled through my pockets for something to stem the flow; all I could find was a letter about the *HMS Belfast* trip (packed lunch, a maximum of three pounds for the gift shop, no peanut products) and a melted Malteser, so I dabbed at the wound with the end of my tie.

And then I smelled vinegar. 'Hang on . . .' My regulation blue-and-white St Thomas's tie appeared to have developed a red stripe. When I explored it with the tip of my tongue, I realised that it wasn't blood at all, it was . . . 'Huh . . . Tomato sauce.'

I can't tell you what a relief that was. There was supposed to be a ceasefire, but the Year Nine Ketchup Wars had obviously broken out again; just my luck to get caught in the crossfire.

But the feeling of relief lasted about two seconds. Callum Corcoran was grinning like a children's telly presenter and waving his finger at my head.

'Look at him. Ha, ha, ha, ha, ha, ha, ha. What's the matter, Sam? Not your time of the month is it? Didn't think you'd reached puberty yet!'

Animal had cracked up the moment he heard the phrase 'time of the month'.

My face froze when I attempted a smile. 'I just . . . Well I was . . . ' If I didn't get out of there fast, I had every chance of becoming 'the boy who cried'.

Callum advanced menacingly, brandishing a loaded can of Diet Coke. 'Eh, Sam, got any more jokes?'

'Yeah,' said Animal, 'tell us another one.'

I reached frantically under the table for my rucksack. 'No, soz I —'

'Come on,' said Callum, 'we was only having a laugh.'

If I hadn't been in such a hurry to get the hell out of there I might have spotted the rogue PE kit that wrapped itself around my ankle and sent me plummeting to the ground like that footballer Alex was so keen on. I crawled the last few metres to the door, stumbling gratefully into the corridor, wishing I was a Time Lord who could just hop in the Tardis and jump forward to half past three. But like Granddad was always saying, 'You should be careful what you wish for.'

3.30 p.m.
'All aboard for the Skylark,' shouted Barry the Bus Driver as the Year Elevens swarmed up the steps. 'No spitting, kicking, biting or eye-gouging. Flick-knives and Kalashnikovs are strictly forbidden. And may the best young gentleman – or young lady – win.'

iPod blasting 'Mood Indigo' (the 1930 recording), I hovered in the bushes until they were all in their seats. It might have looked pretty random, but everyone knew their place. From Callum's older brother Luke and his spotty mates in the back row, past Gaz Lulham and Pete Hughes in the middle, right through to me, Alex and a couple of Year Seven girls at the front, the pecking order was as well established as Mum's chicken coop, and woe betide the hapless hen who tried to step out of line.

A brief moment of calm descended as mobile phones were produced and messages checked. I slipped up the stairs and flopped down next to Alex.

'*Is anyone watching me?*'

'No need to shout. What are you listening to anyway? Not that jazz stuff again?'

'Is anyone watching me?'

'What's the matter with you? You've been acting weird all afternoon.'

'Just have a quick look, will you? Is someone staring at me?'

Alex glanced towards the back of the bus. 'Oh . . . my . . . *God*!'

'What.'

'Luke Corcoran's got a huge pair of binoculars, and he's like pointing them straight at you.'

Lex hadn't laughed like that since the time we made a prank call to the I Can't Believe It's Not Butter helpline. 'It's not that funny.'

Barry the Bus Driver pulled down his shades and did his usual Elvis Presley impression over the PA system: 'Thankyouverymuch, ladies and gentlemen. Now, will you kindly fasten your safety belts?'

'You sure no one's staring at me?'

'Why would anyone want to do that?'

'Doesn't matter,' I said, relaxing slightly, but sliding further down my seat just in case. 'At least I . . .'

Alex smiled and started texting. 'You going online later?'

'Doubt it . . . got clarinet practice.'

'Why not? It only takes like three minutes, doesn't it?'

For some reason, I didn't want to tell him about the night before. 'Yeah . . . well . . . anyway, how about you?'

'Probably not. Mum's so upset about Dad's new girl-friend she wants us all to watch a DVD together.'

I had a chilling vision of Alex cowering behind the sofa during the more disturbing moments of *High School Musical*. 'Cheer up; your dad'll soon get fed up with her.'

'Nah,' he said gloomily, 'this one's different.'

I tried hard not to laugh. 'Yeah, right.'

'He reckons he loves her,' said Alex, his texting thumb going into overdrive.

'If you ask me, it'll all be over by Christmas.'

'Well, I didn't, did I?'

It was no good trying to reason with him when he was like that. Lex could be quite unreasonable when he made his mind up about something. So, I turned up the volume of 'It Aint What You Do (It's The Way That You Do It)' and tried to remember what I was supposed to be getting for Granddad. With any luck, he might even let me in on that secret of his.

I was feeling much more like my old self. The incident in the canteen would be a funny story to tell Granddad, and I'd not had another text message since PSHE. Perhaps it was all over.

It had only just begun.

Two minutes before my stop, a paper aeroplane floated overhead and crash-landed at my feet. I was about to lob it back when, there on the fuselage, in tiny red letters, I saw the words, *Roses are red, violets are blue, but chickenboyz stink, and we hate you.*

Luv Ollyg78 and The Emperor.

4.05 p.m.

Granddad called it The Departure Lounge, but the sign said *Lavender Lodge*. It didn't smell of lavender though, just boiled cabbage and disinfectant.

'Hello Sam,' said Petal, Granddad's favourite care assistant. 'Why don't you come down to the kitchen and I'll fix you a nice drink and a Kit Kat?'

'Thanks,' I said, not having the heart to tell her I didn't really like orange squash any more, and Mum said I wasn't allowed to eat Nestlé. (It was something to do with flogging powdered babies' milk to poor people, but as soon as she'd mentioned breast-feeding, I'd decided to take her word for it.)

We passed through a guard of honour of tartan-blanketed old ladies in high-backed chairs, dozing in front of *Countdown*. 'I don't know what's got into that granddad of yours. Tap, tap, tapping away all night he was. Lucky everyone in here's so deaf.'

'What's he up to then?'

Petal shrugged and led me into the kitchen. 'I wish I knew. I've tried torture and everything, but he won't spill the beans.'

My polite smile came out as more of a worried frown.

'Are you all right, Sam? she said, staring hard at me and stroking her double chin. 'You seem a bit . . . subdued.'

'I'm fine, just . . .'

'You can tell me, you know. I won't bite.'

I felt in my trouser pocket for the remains of the scrunched-up paper aeroplane. 'No . . . it's OK.'

28

She handed me a plastic tumbler of pale orange liquid and two fingers of Kit Kat on a stripy saucer. 'Full of secrets your family, aren't they?'

'Are we?'

'Look, if you can't tell me, maybe you should talk to your granddad. He thinks the world of you, you know. Why don't you tell him what's on your mind?'

Granddad was staring at the empty park bench below his window. He'd got that mad look in his eyes. 'He's out there. I know he is!'

'Not this again.'

'Have a quick gander for me, there's a good boy. Now, be honest, is someone watching me?'

I took a quick peek, just to keep him happy. 'No Granddad, no one's watching you.'

'That's all right then.' Quick as a flash he was back to the old granddad I knew and loved. 'Now, what have you got for me?'

'You're lucky, it was the last one.'

'Good lad. I knew you wouldn't let me down.'

We shook hands. Granddad didn't approve of the 'twenty-first century mania for public displays of male affection'. He used to totally crush me, but ever since his 'funny turn' in Specsavers, his grip had been much gentler. 'How are you feeling, Granddad?'

'Oh you know,' he said, hobbling over to the bookcase for cutlery, 'still sitting up and taking punishment.'

He was about twenty years older than Alex's granddad,

but even though he was practically prehistoric, we still found plenty to talk about. I spotted his old-fashioned typewriter on the dressing table and the wastepaper basket overflowing with rolled-up sheets of A4. 'You been writing to the paper again, Granddad?'

He shook his head and set about dividing the pork pie that I'd just bought him into triangles. 'Not this time, m'boy.'

He'd always got a letter in the *County Times*. The last one was to complain about the *Five Items or Less* sign in the supermarket (. . . *when, as every schoolboy knows, it should read, Five Items or Fewer*).

'Petal says you were typing all night.'

'I can't tell you how much I've been looking forward to this,' he said, savouring the first mouthful. 'The food in here is worse than Pompey Barracks.'

'It's not something to do with that . . . *thing* you were going to tell me is it?'

'Shhh . . . someone might hear you.'

'So it is then?'

'Can't a man enjoy a pork pie in peace for once? Now why don't you take a seat, and as soon as I've consumed this magnificent delicacy, I might just think about enlightening you.'

Granddad's lumpy bed squealed with pain as I sank into the patchwork quilt that Nanny had made during her last stay in hospital. Sometimes I played a mental game of I-Spy, trying to spot stuff from their old house in Brighton: the African figures that Granddad got from the Ju-ju man,

Nanny's collection of miniature teapots, a picture of Dad when he still had hair, and that painting of the Palace Pier which had hung over the fireplace in the little back bedroom that I'd slept in when I went to visit.

Granddad belched contently and heaved himself to his feet. 'It's something I've never told anyone, Sam, not even your grandmother.'

'But what is it?'

His old bones creaked terribly as he bent down in front of the dressing table and pulled open the bottom drawer. 'I didn't think I'd be able to tell you without . . . ' He took out a tatty, blue ring-binder and tried to kick the drawer closed with his carpet slippers. 'That is, I thought you might understand better if I wrote it all down.'

'Understand what?'

He collapsed onto his chair, letting out a wheeze of relief. 'Here, you'd better take this before I change my mind.'

Sellotaped to the front of the folder was a fading photograph of three men in white sailors' uniforms. And underneath the title, *Sliding Off the Edge of the World*, a short note beginning *Dear Sam* in Granddad's spidery handwriting.

'Who are those guys?' I said, noticing that there were at least twenty pages and wondering if he was expecting me to read them all.

'That handsome devil on the left is yours truly.'

'But where's your war wound?' (Granddad had a cool Action Man scar below his left eye.)

'This picture was taken in Alexandria. A couple of days before we . . . before we . . . '

Sometimes he got all choked up when he talked about the war.

'What about the other two?'

'That's Sharky Beal,' he said, his finger trembling above the bushy-eyed sailor with a sad look in his eyes. 'He had a bit of a temper on him, if you know what I mean. And the one in the middle, that's my old oppo Tommy, Tommy Riley.'

'Old oppo?'

'It's the naval term for best mate. Tommy was a Norwich lad. We hit it off from the start. 'Course, it probably helped that the very first time we met he saved me from a thrashing.'

The man in the middle had a shy smile and sticky-out ears. 'He looks really wicked.'

'Yes,' said Granddad, not even bothering to tell me off for saying 'wicked'. 'I didn't deserve a friend like Tommy.'

Either his eyes were watering more than usual or that was a tear sliding off the edge of his face. I had this strange vision of Dad warning him not to cry on his first day at the old people's home.

'How come it's such a big secret, Granddad?'

'I think you'd better be the judge of that, m'boy. All I want is to set the record straight.'

'But why now? I don't understand.'

'They've called my flight, Sam.'

'What do you . . . ?' And then I realised what he meant.

32

'No, Granddad . . . *No*, it's not true, it can't be!'

He nodded gravely. 'I don't need some quack to tell me I'm on the way out. As soon as I started dreaming about him again, I knew my number was up.'

'Dreaming about who?'

'Never mind that; just read the damned thing, just read it before it's too late.'

Mum had warned me that old people could suddenly go 'doolally' without any warning.

'You've got to tell Dad about this. He worries about you, you know. Why not give him a ring on that phone he gave you?'

'He knows where I am,' said Granddad, sounding as on the ball as ever. 'He should do,' he added bitterly. 'After all, he's the one who put me here.'

'Yes but what if —?'

'Just read it, Sam. Then you'll know who I really am.'

'But I love you as you are, Granddad.'

'All secrets are lies – you know that, don't you? They gnaw away at your insides, like cancer, until you can't stand it any longer. And this one's been playing havoc with my guts for the last sixty years. You will read it, won't you, m'boy?'

I stuffed the blue ring-binder into my rucksack. ''Course I will, Granddad.'

He smiled and gave me a naval salute. 'Good lad. Now, if you don't mind, it's probably time you were buggering off. I don't know how many episodes of *The Weakest Link* I've got left, and your mother will be expecting you.'

'I'll see you next week then,' I said, slinging my rucksack over my shoulder. Halfway to the door, another question popped into my head. 'Why me, Granddad?'

'Because we share the same genes,' he said, scrabbling around in the bottom of his armchair (just like I did) looking for the remote, 'because I'll always be a part of you. Your father grew up thinking I was a bit of a hero. Perhaps when you know the truth about me, Sam, you'll be able to understand yourself a bit better.'

It sounded like the sort of thing Mum would say to one of her 'clients'. But I was more concerned about that other thing he'd said – that thing about all secrets being lies. I so should have told him, I know that now. But what would a man with a war wound, a man who'd fought for his country, a man who'd looked death in the face and survived, what would he have thought of me if I'd told him I was totally terrified about going back to school on Monday? So I decided to leave him with a joke instead.

'Hey Granddad, did you know diarrhoea is hereditary?'

7.28 p.m.
'Mind if I ask you something, Britney?' I said, holding her tightly so she couldn't wriggle. 'Do you ever feel like someone's watching you?'

She cackled gently and nodded.

'What a stupid question. Of course you do. Are you still having nightmares about that rotten F-O-X?'

I knew that chickens couldn't spell, but they're sensitive

34

creatures and Britney had never been the same since Mother Theresa was savaged by the fox. Miss Piggy, Tracey (Beaker) and Madonna hardly noticed the old bird had gone. It was only Britney who seemed to take it to heart. That's why she was my favourite. I could talk to Britney.

'You won't believe what a terrible day I've had. Listen to this. It's been running round my head ever since I read it: *Roses are red, violets are blue, but chickenboyz stink, and we hate you.* Horrible isn't it? They sent me a text too. What do they want, Britney? What are they trying to do?'

I placed her back on the perch and started the disgusting process of scraping chicken poo from the droppings tray and collecting it in Mum's compost bin. Turning Dad's shed into a chicken coop had sounded like a bit of a laugh until she told me who was expected to clean it out every week. I was supposed to do it after school on Tuesday, but Lex and I had been to that new LaserQuest in town, and I thought Mum had forgotten about it until I saw the dreaded rubber gloves on the kitchen table.

'Even Granddad's acting all strange. He keeps saying he's dying. That can't be right, can it?'

I was expected to check the poo to make sure it was healthy (it should be brown with a little white cap) but to tell you the truth, it smelled so terrible I always closed my eyes and held my breath.

'And he's given me this story thingy to read. What's up with him, do you think? I couldn't stand it if anything happened to Granddad. He's about the best friend I've got at the moment – apart from you, of course, Britney.'

I snapped closed the compost bin and sucked in a deep breath. 'Right, I'll just check the nesting boxes and I'm out of here.'

That was strange. It wasn't unusual for one of them to stop laying for a day or so, but it was quite unheard of for all four of them not to produce a single egg. 'What's the matter, girls, not on strike, are we?'

I rooted around in the cosy little nesting boxes, sinking my hand into the tepid straw, just in case I'd missed one. I hadn't of course; they were as empty as Callum Corcoran's homework diary. It was what Granddad would have called 'one of life's little mysteries'. So why was I as jittery as Britney? Why did it feel like even the chickens had it in for me?

7.40 p.m.
'Done it,' I shouted, chucking my rubber gloves in the kitchen sink and walking into the lounge.

'Did you remember to put out some new grit?'

'Yes, Mum.'

'And what's my compost like?'

'Smelly.'

'Good. How many eggs were there?'

I flopped down next to her on the sofa. 'There weren't any.'

'What?'

'I double-checked and everything.'

'Oh dear,' said Mum, spreading her papers across the coffee table. 'Maybe that wretched fox is back.'

'Yes, maybe.'

'Well, that's a double first then.' She smiled. 'No eggs *and* you haven't dashed straight upstairs to commune with your beloved computer. What's got into you?'

'*Nothing*, I just thought I'd stay down here and keep you company.'

'You haven't broken something, have you?'

She still hadn't forgiven Alex and me for using her bra to fire tennis balls at next-door's cat.

'No, Mum.'

'OK then,' she said, pulling me towards her and pressing her face into my hair. 'But we're not having the goggle box on – not until *Midsomer Murders* anyway. I've got work to do. There's something about this child I'm seeing that doesn't quite add up. When you've been doing the job as long as I have, you begin to develop a sort of sixth sense.'

'It's all right, Mum. I'm going to read some of Granddad's thing.'

'What is it anyway?'

'Dunno really, but from the way he was talking, you'd think it was a matter of life or death.'

'Now why doesn't that surprise me?' She studied the photo on the front cover. 'That's him there, isn't it? Ah, doesn't he look like your dad – except with more hair of course!' She stared wistfully at the picture of the three sailors, but I knew who she was really thinking about. Dad

37

had been on the Hardman tour for four weeks, three days, five hours and twenty minutes, and although she kept on saying, 'If you love someone, let them go,' I reckon she was missing him even more than I was. 'Anyway . . . let's get on, shall we?'

Granddad's story was full of pencil markings and underlinings, and spattered with that white stuff that he used to cover up mistakes. And I was pretty sure that was a marmalade stain. I slid up the sofa towards Mum until our legs were touching, and started reading.

Dear Sam,

Time is a notorious thief. Everything I want to tell you about actually happened, but you must forgive me if, after more than sixty years, my memory fails me on a few of the finer details. Should you come across any schoolboy howlers, I hope it will bring you as much satisfaction as I have gleaned from spotting historical inaccuracies in BBC costume dramas (never enough horse dung on the streets).

Please don't judge me too harshly. Believe me, I have already done that myself.

'Illegitimi nil carborundum.'

Your loving Granddad

Sliding Off
the Edge of the World

PADDINGTON STATION, MAY 1943

Two days before my eighteenth birthday my tearful mother presented me with a brown envelope marked ON HIS MAJESTY'S SERVICE OFFICIAL PAID. Inside was a one-way railway voucher, a postal order for two shillings, a letter instructing me to report to HMS Raleigh, the naval training base in Plymouth, and a stern warning that failure to do so would result in my being classed as a deserter.

A week later, I was sitting in a jam-packed, third-class railway compartment, along with half a dozen snoring squaddies (they'd even commandeered the luggage rack as a makeshift hammock), a couple of Wrens (Women's Royal Naval Service) and a few nervous youngsters in civvies, like me.

I was already pining for Mum's Yorkshire pudding when the train juddered forward and a cheery face appeared at the open window. A fellow with thick bushy eyebrows and a green canvas suitcase was trotting down the platform alongside me.

'Oi, mate,' he said. 'This one going to Plymouth, is it?'

I told him it was.

This was wartime remember, Sam. No one turned a hair when a green suitcase flew through the window followed by the out-stretched figure of its owner screaming, 'Geronimo!'

He dusted himself down and squeezed in next to me. 'Sharky Beal's the name. Sharky from Shoreditch, pleased to meet yer.'

We soon established we were both bound for HMS Raleigh and, for a while at least, the journey passed pleasantly enough. I'm not sure what we talked about, but I do recall being somewhat surprised by his almost unnatural enthusiasm for the battles to come. 'All I want's to see some action,' he kept on saying. 'Make my family proud.'

Things took a turn for the worse when I asked him what I thought was a perfectly innocent question: 'You said you were from Shoreditch, Sharky. That's in the East End, isn't it?'

'Well, it's not bleedin' Mayfair.'

'Me and my mum were there in '41.'

'I thought you was a Brighton lad.'

'I am. We only went up for the day.'

His eyebrows moved even closer together. 'What, like trippers you mean?'

I told him we'd wanted to see the Blitz damage for ourselves; how a friendly shop-keeper had directed us to the worst scenes of devastation; how shocked we'd been by the rows of houses with their fronts blown clean off, the huge craters in the middle of the road and the dreadful smell of burning.

'Ruin your holiday, did it?'

I tried to protest, but he grabbed me by the collar and lifted me clean out of my seat. 'You thought you'd come and do a bit of sightseeing, didn't yer? I ought to knock

41

your block off.'

And that's exactly what he would have done, had not a disembodied voice stopped him dead in his tracks. 'I wouldn't do that if I were you.'

Sharky hesitated, his fist hovering above me like the sword of Damocles.

The News Chronicle in the corner appeared to have developed the power of speech. 'I said, I wouldn't do that if I were you. Not unless you want a murder on your conscience.'

Sharky relaxed his fist. 'Murder? What do you mean murder?'

The chap in the corner lowered his newspaper, revealing a youthful countenance and an unusually voluminous pair of ears. 'That man has psychotalclapsica.'

'Hang on a tick, Professor,' said Sharky. 'Psychotalwhatsica?'

'A very serious condition,' continued the man with The Chronicle. 'One blow to the cranium is all it would take.'

Sharky looked doubtful. 'You a doctor or something?'

'Not exactly,' said the young chap, reaching into his pocket for a packet of boiled sweets, 'but I know enough about physiognomy to realise what a risk you're taking.'

'Answer me this then, Professor,' said Sharky. 'If he's got the dreaded lurgie, how come he's off to do his bit? HMS Raleigh ain't going to be no holiday camp, you know.'

'Same reason as you and me, I should think. He's just got his call-up papers. I daresay with his condition he could have wangled himself a cushy desk job, but he didn't, did he? I'd say that makes him a bit of a hero, wouldn't you?'

I was so grateful I could almost have hugged him.

'All right,' said Sharky, still not looking entirely convinced, 'just this once, I'll let you off.' An angry King Kong became the friendly face at the window again. 'Looks like we'll be shipmates, Professor; what's your name anyway?'

'It's Tommy,' said my jug-eared protector. 'Tommy Riley.'

8.00 p.m.

The *Mission: Impossible* theme took a sledgehammer to the silence. Mum looked up grumpily from her notes. 'Aren't you going to answer that, Samuel? It might be your father.'

'It's only a text,' I said, sliding to the other end of the sofa, and scrolling through the menu, 'so it can't be Dad because he doesn't even know how to send one.'

Mum looked disappointed. 'Who's it from then?'

I glanced down at the message, trying to shield it from her whilst surreptitiously storing the number. 'Oh . . . no one.'

Mum morphed into Child Psychiatrist Person. 'What do you mean exactly by no one?'

'Well, you know . . . ' I said, swiftly returning the mobile to my pocket and trying to suppress the shiver in my voice. 'Just some random guy.'

'Oh, I get it,' said Mum, giving me one of the special smiles she saved for when I wrote something mushy in her Mothers' Day card or Dad gave me the money to buy her a bunch of flowers.

'Get what?'

'I wasn't born yesterday, Sam. I know exactly what's going on.'

It was almost a relief. 'You do?'

'Yes, and I think it's really sweet.'

'Eh?'

'My little boy's got a girlfriend. I'm right, aren't I?' Mum gazed at my eight-year-old self on the mantelpiece, complete with Harry Potter glasses and the scar she drew with a felt tip. She'd got the exact same photo in her office; it was a miracle she didn't get fed up with it. 'My mother was right,' she said dreamily. 'Kids do grow up too fast.'

'No, Mum, you don't under—' And I was just about to reassure her that I found the opposite sex about as interesting as a garden centre, when I suddenly realised that I'd rather she believed her 'little boy' had a girlfriend than that he was scared and unhappy and hadn't a clue how to handle it. 'I mean, it's no big deal, is it?'

'Not to you maybe,' she sniffed. 'But you needn't worry, Sammy, I won't give you a hard time about it.'

'Thanks, Mum.'

She fiddled with her papers, drummed on the coffee table and whistled the theme tune from *Casualty*. 'Aren't you going to text her back then?'

'No, Mum. I've got to read some more of this. I'll do it later.'

'Treat 'em mean and keep 'em keen, eh? Just like your dad.'

Everyone in my family seemed to be some kind of a hero – everyone except, me that is. My great-granddad fought in the trenches, Dad was a semi-professional Hardman, and Granddad even had a war wound. I tried to concentrate on his story, hoping that perhaps some of his bravery would rub off on me, but all I could see was a load of squiggly lines, like that painting Mum was so keen on in the Tate Modern.

What was the point? My mind kept wandering back to my mobile. And although I pretended to carry on reading for Mum's benefit, it was only to put off the fateful moment when I'd have to go upstairs and there would be nothing to stop me rereading that terrible text.

9.25 p.m.
'Come on, love; I'm sure your granddad's life history is all very interesting – *not!* But you really should go up and get ready for bed. I know you're dying to phone your new girl-friend.'

'Do I have to?'

'Of course you do. Faint heart never won fair lady, Sammy.'

'OK then,' I said, wracking my brains for another reason not be left alone with my mobile. 'Oh and Mum?'

'Yes.'

'No one does that "not" thing any more.'

'Well, pardon me for being such an embarrassment.'

She'd spent the last hour rearranging her notes on the coffee table. It reminded me of that thing Granddad had once said about people rearranging the deck chairs on the *Titanic* as it went down.

'How's that difficult case of yours? Have you worked it out yet, Mum?'

'Not really. It'll be one of the three Ds, of course – drink, daddies and divorce – but I've never seen a child so full of hate. I just wish I could help.'

'Here, why don't you let me have a look?'

'*No,*' she said, gathering her papers into a pile like a gambler collecting his winnings, 'you mustn't.'

'Why not?'

'Just . . . because. Now hurry up and get a move on.'

I headed reluctantly for the door. 'Mum?'

'What is it, love? Is something the matter?'

'It's just . . . ' It was no good; I couldn't tell her. She got so upset when she thought I was unhappy. ' . . . I love you.'

'I love you too, you soppy thing. But it's still bedtime, Sammy, so get up those stairs!'

I didn't see them at first. I was too busy trying not to think about that text. But when I looked out at the bus shelter, I got the shock of my life.

They haven't . . . have they?

The feeling that I was being watched grew stronger with every step towards my bedroom window. Five droopy yellow eyes, weeping sticky tears and shattered eggshells, were staring in at me, following me around the room like Big Brother. Unless Mr Fox had learned to throw, he was probably in the clear.

I yanked closed the curtains, trying to pretend that the glutinous concoction of broken eggs sliding down my windowpane wasn't there. It wasn't the only thing I was doing my best to forget about. How much longer could I keep it up? Sooner or later, I'd have to bite the bullet.

I padded around my bedroom like a caged animal, tearing the last three days off my *Far Side* calendar, strumming every chord I knew on the guitar (E minor and A minor), and pausing to admire the original *Star Wars* poster that Dad had bought me in Greenwich market, before logging onto the laptop and Googling *HMS Belfast* – anything to avoid getting out my mobile.

The virtual tour was actually pretty cool, but after a couple of minutes exploring the lower decks (you could even go right down to the engine rooms), I knew I couldn't put it off any longer. Gritting my teeth, I reached for the Dad Phone and went straight to my inbox.

Ever been so desperate for something not to be true that you kind of convinced yourself it was a mistake, even though it couldn't be? When the specialist told him what was wrong with Nanny, Granddad said he'd managed to pretend it was just a 'gippy tummy' for weeks. And there I was, vainly hoping that I'd misread it, or started hallucinating even – like Dad after his first double marathon.

But I couldn't ignore the evidence of my own eyes. It was right there, in black and white, just as I'd remembered it.

Check out www.chickenboyz.com
With hate – The Emperor

10.30 p.m.
Ever stood at the top of a cliff and half wanted to throw yourself off? That's what it felt like; only this time, instead of stepping back from the precipice, I knew that – even if I spent another twenty minutes staring at my Grade Three clarinet certificate – sooner or later, I'd have to jump.

I typed in the address and prepared myself for the worst.

I wasn't sure what to expect, but it was far worse than

anything I could possibly have imagined. At first, all you heard was the music – it was that 'Birdie Song' Mum and Dad had done a really embarrassing dance to at Auntie Deb's wedding – and then a flash animation of a person in a chicken suit waddled across the screen shaking its butt at you like Baloo the Bear. Everyone in Year Eight was into flash animation. The boys used it to make films of random acts of violence and the girls did cartoon frogs sticking their tongues out to catch flies.

And I was almost enjoying it until the chicken turned round and I saw that he was carrying a clarinet case. On the side, in graffiti-style lettering, were the words, *Click on my beak to see the dumbest kid in Year Eight.*

I held my breath; reaching for the mouse with a cold, clammy hand.

'Oh no,' I whispered. 'It can't be?'

There in the top left-hand corner of the home page was a picture of me, trying to do the Fosbury Flop. I'd hated that PE lesson. I mean, why would anyone try to jump over something backwards? No wonder I'd kept knocking the bar off.

But there was worse to come – much worse. Underneath the photograph was:

THE EMPEROR'S BLOG

Hi. Welcome to a cool new website dedicated to Sam Tennant, aka Chickenboy, aka the most pathetic kid at St Thomas's Community College. If you hate and despise him half as much as we do, then this is the site for you.

And remember to tell all your friends. If you want to be ahead of the game, why not sign up for regular 'Chickenboyz' updates to your mobile.

Enjoy!

PS: If you really want to see some fun, don't forget your *HMS Belfast* money on Monday. You can run, Sam, but you can't hide!

So it was true then, I couldn't deny it any longer – someone at school actually hated me. No, not just one person, two at least – on the other side of the page was a column entitled:

FIVE REALLY GAY THINGS ABOUT SAM TENNANT
by Ollyg78

1. He thinks he's really funny but he's not.
2. He likes crap music. (Ask Chickenboy what's on his iPod!)
3. He smells of chicken poo.
4. His mum smells of chicken poo.
5. He's a scaredy little chicken who deserves everything he gets.

I thought I was going to be sick. How could anyone hate me that much? What had I done? And who was he, this Emperor, I mean? Thank goodness it was Friday. I'd have the whole weekend to figure it out. If I could just do that, perhaps I'd be able to put things right – apologise or something. I was halfway through dialling Alex's number, to see if he'd got any ideas, when I realised that I didn't really want my best friend to know about it. So I started running through a mental list of suspects, beginning with the obvious one – beginning with Callum Corcoran.

'You're not still on that computer, are you?'

'Mum! You made me jump.' What was that she'd always said about knocking first?

'What are you up to anyway?'

'Nothing,' I said, doing my best to create a human wall between Mum and the screen.

'Oh come off it. I know you've been chatting to your girlfriend. Two more minutes max and then bed.'

I stabbed hastily at the keyboard. 'It's OK, Mum, I've logged off.'

'I *can* just about remember what it's like, you know,' she said dreamily. 'Your first love's one of the most magical times of your life. Make sure you enjoy it.' Her tight embrace almost squeezed the life out of me. 'Sleep well, Sammy.'

Some hope!

12.47 a.m.

'Come on, Britney, think. You must have seen something. Were there two of them? Did they say anything about me?'

Tracy Beaker and Miss Piggy were sleeping peacefully. Only Britney seemed to appreciate the full gravity of the situation. She was making that funny growling noise and looked every bit as wide-awake as I was.

'Shhh, you'll wake Mum.'

I held her close, enjoying the comforting bundle of warmth against my ancient Chief Wiggum pyjamas.

'OK, here's the way I see it. Callum Corcoran might just about be able to animate a guy blowing his brains out, but could he really manage a dancing chicken? OK, so maybe Animal did it for him. No, that doesn't sound right. Then how about Gaz Lulham?'

Britney wasn't giving anything away.

'Wait a minute, hear me out. When we did that reproduction project, Gaz made a really funny film about a sperm with a hand grenade. He could *easily* have done it . . . Yeah, but Gaz and I were at nursery together. I know he never talks to me at school, but he always nods and grunts if I pass him in town and he's not with his mates.'

Britney didn't look at all impressed with my powers of deduction.

'Well, have you got any better ideas? Who *is* this Emperor . . . and what about Ollyg78? If I could only identify them, I might be able to come up with a plan. What am I going to do, Britney? What am I going to do?'

Her beady eyes met mine. She didn't need to say anything, it was obvious what she was thinking: *You know what to do, Sam. It's what you've been planning all along. I mean, who's the chicken here, you or me?*

The Dad Phone felt like a block of ice against my heart. I slipped it from my pyjama pocket and went straight to the address book – that way I didn't have time to chicken out. And there it was: The Emperor's number.

My thumb twitched like a Gameboy addict's, and it took all my concentration to bring it down on the keypad. 'OK, Britney, this is it.'

I was totally unprepared for what happened next.

Oh no . . . *oh no* . . . it couldn't be, could it?

It was past midnight. I was expecting to go straight through to voicemail. All I'd wanted was to listen to his answerphone message. Fear turned to abject horror the moment I realised that somebody was actually on the other end. 'Hello,' I whispered. 'Hello . . . hello, who is that please?'

Silence, punctuated only by the sound of heavy breathing.

'Please,' I said, squeezing Britney even tighter, 'just tell me who you are and . . . and what you want from me.'

First a crackle, next a hiss, followed by a familiar voice – it sounded just like the posh newsreader guy that Dad used to listen to when Mum had forgotten to turn on Radio One. But it wasn't The Emperor.

'*And now the Shipping Forecast issued by the Met Office, on behalf of the Maritime and Coastguard Agency . . .*'

'Look, this isn't funny,' I shouted. 'Who are you and why are you doing this?'

'*Biscay: North-easterly four or five, becoming variable three in . . .*'

'Who *are* you?'

At least now we knew who the chicken was. I couldn't stop myself; the tears were cascading down my cheeks and making craters in the sawdust. Dad would have been so ashamed of me. He was always going on about 'the boy who cried'.

The light from the lamppost at the bottom of the garden had given the inside of the shed an otherworldly glow. If I was about to be abducted by aliens, they couldn't have picked a more perfect moment.

'*Shannon: variable four. Moderate, becoming rough later . . .*'

MONDAY
(WEEK TWO)

8.25 a.m.

Mum launched into her usual 'friends of the earth' monologue the moment her foot hit the accelerator. I caught the occasional word or three, 'torrential rain in the middle of June . . . when is a politician going to have the balls to . . . bloody four-by-fours . . . have these people never heard about carbon footprints?' but I was much too wrapped up in my own problems to worry about global catastrophes.

It had been the worst weekend since we drove Dad to the airport. I didn't dare go into town in case I ran into someone from school, I didn't dare go online for pretty much the exact same reason, and Alex was at Center Parcs with his dad's new girlfriend, so I spent the whole time on the sofa, watching repeats of *Friends* and failing miserably in my desperate attempts to identify The Emperor.

'Aren't you going to get out then? Earth to Samuel, Earth to Sam . . .'

'What?' I said, suddenly coming to my senses and scanning the hill for likely suspects. 'Oh . . . yeah, OK.'

'You look terrible, Sam. You've got great big bags under your eyes.'

'Didn't sleep much last night,' I said, semi-hoping that she'd ask me why.

'Tell me about it! When I first met your father, I didn't sleep for a fortnight.'

And then I spotted Alex. 'Sorry, Mum, gotta go.'

'Good luck with your DT project.'

'Good luck with your borderline dyspraxic.'

The rain hit me like an icy power shower. I grabbed my clarinet from the back seat and set off in hot pursuit. 'Oi, Lex, wait up.'

He turned and stared short-sightedly in my direction. But he couldn't have seen me because a moment later he turned back and started legging it up the hill. And I didn't blame him. One of the weird customs at our school was that, unless you wanted some serious grief, you could never, *ever* wear a coat – not even on a geography field trip to Antarctica.

The good thing about rainy mornings was that there wasn't such a crush at the gates. People arrived in dribs and drabs and went straight to their tutor bases. That was the last thing I wanted to do. Luckily for me I had wind band first break, so I scuttled over to the music block and dumped my clarinet in the music store, knowing I'd be safe for ten minutes.

Apart from a couple of kids on their way to private instrumental lessons, it was usually pretty deserted at that time of the morning. The high windows meant that you couldn't see out onto the playground, and the long, curvy corridor flickered fluorescently twenty four/seven. I often made a special trip to the music block toilets. They were so much cleaner than the ones outside the Community Reception, and they never ran out of paper.

I locked myself into a graffiti-free cubicle and sat with my head in my hands listening to the distant drone of Miss Hoolyhan's Buddhist chanting in one of the practice rooms. I was praying no one had seen that website. Or that if they had, they'd have forgotten all about it and when I walked into registration, everything would be back to normal.

Like that was ever going to happen.

8.40 a.m.
It seemed like half of 8SE started squawking the moment I walked through the door. I tried to play along by doing a funny chicken dance, but that only made it worse.

'Ah, Samuel,' said Miss Stanley, squinting at me through her thick frames and stabbing the register with her trusty ballpoint. 'You've decided to join us then.'

'Oi, Chickenboy,' shouted Callum Corcoran, 'show us your giblets!'

'Hey Sam,' came a voice from the back. 'Hope you like scrambled eggs.'

'Cor, what a pong,' said Animal. 'Can I open a window, Miss? Miss, can I open a window?'

'What is the matter now, Tristram?' said Miss Stanley, looking like she was on the verge of another migraine.

'It's Sam Tennant, Miss; he stinks of chicken poo.'

'He gets it off his old lady, Miss,' said Chelsea. 'She stinks of chicken poo, *too*.'

'Ha, ha, ha, ha, ha,' hooted Callum Corcoran. 'That rhymes, Miss. Chicken poo, too.'

'All right, that's enough,' said Miss Stanley. 'I don't know what's got into you this morning. 'Now go and sit down please, Samuel. I want to talk about the curriculum enrichment programme.'

I didn't hear a word she was saying. Dazed and confused as a shell-shock victim, I cowered in front of the whiteboard, waiting for the next volley of abuse, wondering if there was anyone in 8SE who hadn't seen that website.

'Did you hear me, Samuel?'

'What, Miss?'

I was used to people laughing *with* me, but I'd never had them laughing *at* me before.

'I said go and sit down. What's the matter with you today?'

And then I saw that my usual place between Gaz and Alex was taken. Gaz must have moved up one – or the other way round of course. The only seat left was right next to Stephen Allbright, the class freak. I death-marched towards it, making a point of not returning Dimbo's sickly smile as I sat down beside him.

'Never mind, Dimbo,' shouted Animal. 'You'll get used to the smell.'

'Look, *please*,' said Miss Stanley, who was always a bit grouchy on Monday mornings. 'I don't want any more of this silly name calling. It's not funny, OK?'

But even I couldn't help noticing the way she transformed into a simpering pussycat the moment the door opened.

'Look, Miss,' said Chelsea. 'It's your boyfriend, Miss.'

'Yes, thank you, Chelsea,' said Mr Catchpole, his face not quite acquiring the same shade of crimson as Miss Stanley's. 'I'll do the funnies.'

Miss Stanley took off her glasses. Her voice was about two octaves lower than before. 'Ah, Mr Catchpole, what can I do for you?

It was as rare as Halley's Comet to see the two most miserable teachers in the school smiling simultaneously. 'I've just come to see how many of this bunch of reprobates have remembered their *HMS Belfast* money.'

A forest of hands reached for the sky; my heart set off in the opposite direction.

'Well, well,' said Mr Catchpole, 'that's a turn up for the books. I wonder what's brought about this sudden *volte-face*.'

Pete Hughes was usually far too cool to put his hand up. He had the best haircut in Year Eight, a girlfriend in Year Nine, plus which he was probably the only kid in the tutor group (apart from me and Stephen Allbright) who knew what *volte-face* meant. 'We saw this really interesting website, Mr Catchpole, Sir.' He grinned. 'We all thought that going round an old ship would be as bad as listening to Mr Peel's band, but now we know we're really going to see some fun, Sir. Now we're looking forward to it.'

'I'm pleased to hear it,' said Mr Catchpole, smoothing the lapels of his Marks & Spencer jacket. 'I'm quite looking forward to it myself. How about you, Miss Stanley?'

'Oh yes, Mr Catchpole, can't wait.'

It looked like I was the only person in the room who was dreading it. I screwed my eyes tight shut and bit hard on my bottom lip. What were the chances of me making it through to first break without crying? Fat and slim, I'd have said.

And I was desperately trying to hold it together when another thought hit me thwack between the eyes: Didn't Pete Hughes once tell me he had his own website? Didn't Pete Hughes just quote almost directly from Chickenboyz.com? He was certainly cool enough to animate dancing poultry. Supposing it was him – supposing Pete Hughes was The Emperor?

10.57 a.m.

Mum and Dad were always telling me that I'd never regret learning a musical instrument. For the first time in my life, I knew exactly what they meant. If Mum hadn't bullied me into practising every other blue moon, I would have been trying to avoid Callum and his mates in the canteen, or pretending to ignore the chicken noises that followed me everywhere, instead of sitting in the music block rehearsal studio miming to 'Waterloo' while the wind band murdered ABBA's greatest hits. For twenty-five minutes, I was safe. For twenty-five minutes, I knew that The Emperor (whoever *he* was) couldn't get at me.

Miss Hoolyhan drew enormous smiley faces in the air with her baton and sang along to 'Waterloo', like one of the joke contestants on *X Factor*.

Abby could actually play it too. I think she was like Grade Five or something. Maybe when you were as quiet as she was, playing the clarinet was a good way of avoiding having to talk too much. (That's the sort of thing Mum would have said anyway.) But who cared why she did it if it meant I didn't have to play a note? Right at the moment, all I could think about was what on earth The Emperor was going to do next.

'That wasn't *quite* right, was it, guys?' said Miss Hoolyhan charitably. 'Let's hear the flutes and maracas from bar one hundred and eight.'

Right at that moment, all I wanted to do was curl up into a ball and go to sleep until it was all over.

'Are you OK?'

'What?'

Abby took a pink paper tissue from her shoulder bag and smiled sympathetically. I couldn't help wondering if it was difficult to play with all that junk in your mouth. 'Here,' she said, 'you look like you could do with it.'

'What do you mean?'

'Come on, Sam,' she whispered. 'I know you're crying. I do it all the time at home. Here, take it.'

'Thanks.' Having someone being kind to me was the last straw. I'd managed to hold back all morning, but the flood-gates had finally opened. 'Sorry, I . . .'

Abby put her hand on my shoulder. I was slightly surprised at her non-regulation fingernails. 'Don't worry, Sam. I won't tell anyone – promise.'

I nodded gratefully and dabbed my eyes with her tissue.

'It's about that nasty website, isn't it?' she said, angrily. 'I saw it on Friday night.'

'How did you find out about it?'

'Someone texted me. I was expecting a funny video clip or something.'

'Who is he, Abby? Who's The Emperor?'

'I don't know, Sam. I don't think anyone does. But I'll try and find out for you.'

'Thanks.'

'I think it's pathetic the way The Emperor's turned that lot against you. Talk about the herd instinct.' She leaned towards me. I felt her warm breath in my ear. 'Promise me you'll be careful, Sam.'

I'd never noticed her freckles; all I'd seen before was the brace. 'Do you think I need to be careful?'

'I hope not, Sam. But if you ever want to talk about it, you can always talk to me.' She smiled to herself, as if she'd just remembered something funny. 'Talking is so much better than letting things fester inside, you know.'

'Right,' said Miss Hoolyhan, obviously beginning to regret appointing a maracas player with no sense of rhythm, 'let's all go from bar one hundred and eight. One, two, three, and . . .'

And although ninety-nine per cent of me was already worrying about where I was going to hide in second break, a bizarre thought had just popped into the back of my head: If I ever *did* have a girlfriend (and it was the mother of all ifs, believe me) I'd want her to be a bit like Abby.

1.28 p.m.
Two minutes to second break and I couldn't believe how lucky I'd been. Apart from the occasional squawking sound and Gaz Lulham's crack about headless chickens, the only thing I'd had to deal with was burned shortbread – and it might have been me who'd set the timer wrong anyway.

All that was about to change.

Mr Peel, who had this pathetic fantasy that he was 'down with the kids', suddenly broke off from the Peasants' Revolt and started droning on about The Arctic Monkeys. 'It's what I call the democratisation of the media. A band puts a track on the net, yeah, and some faceless suit doesn't decide if it's a phat vibe – *you* do. And that's the way it should be.'

'Guess what Sam Tennant's got on his iPod, Sir,' said Pete Hughes.

'Let's see now,' said Mr Peel, stroking his goatee. 'The Wombats . . . Lily Allen . . . Maybe an old warhorse like The Ramones?'

Pete Hughes smirked triumphantly. 'Glenn Miller, Sir.'

'Yeah,' said Chelsea. 'What a loser. No wonder The

Emperor hates his guts.'

Mr Peel looked genuinely concerned. 'Sorry, Pete, never heard of them. Are they an R 'n' B combo or what?'

'No, Sir, Glenn Miller, Sir,' said Pete Hughes. 'The wartime bandleader, Sir? We did him in music. He wrote 'In the Mood'? *Da da da da da da da da da da da da da.*'

Mr Peel looked mightily relieved. 'Yeah, nice one.' And despite the fact that I didn't even like Glenn Miller, he was still chuckling when the bell went. 'Don't forget guys,' he shouted after us as the stampede began, 'if you want to check out my new demo, just Google "Robot Can-Can Dancers" and follow the links.'

I made a mad dash for the door, but someone beat me to it. It was Alex. He shot down the humanities corridor like a rat up a drainpipe.

'Hey, Lex, hang on a minute, I really need to talk to you.'

Just as I was closing in on him, the others burst out of the history room and Pete Hughes started an encore of 'In the Mood'.

'Come on, Alex, I thought we were mates.'

'Stop following me,' he hissed. 'I can't talk right now.'

'Then when *can* you talk? You've been avoiding me all day.'

His ears were practically illuminating the corridor. 'I dunno . . . sorry . . . gotta go.'

'What's wrong? What are you scared of?

But Alex had vanished. He was the one person in the world I thought I could rely on. How wrong can you be?

'Oi, Chickenboy,' yelled a spiteful voice. 'Is it true your

mum's such a bitch that your dad ran away to join a freak show?'

The humanities corridor echoed with their cruel laughter.

I sprinted out to the courtyard, taking the less popular route round the back of the mobile classrooms, and found a handy vantage point behind the drama studio, from where I could spy on everyone going into the canteen. I couldn't hear what Pete Hughes was saying to Callum Corcoran and the others, but I guessed from their toothpaste-advert smiles that it was something about me.

Pete Hughes was the only boy in Year Eight who went for the 'healthy option', but even if it did take the dinner grannies a couple of minutes longer to locate the rabbit food, he'd be out of there in no time. There was only one thing for it: I'd have to find somewhere to hide.

But where? The answer came to me in a flash. Never in my wildest dreams had I imagined myself ending up there. Never in my darkest nightmares had I ever been that desperate.

1.35 p.m.

The Homework Club, or Club Nerd as we called it, was the least popular club in the school. There were lots of stupid myths about the Homework Club (the Nerds were building a time machine so they could go back to 1966 and watch the first episode of *Star Trek*, no one was allowed in without ginger hair and glasses, you had to speak Latin, etc, etc.) but there was certainly an element of truth in the strict code-of-silence thing, because all ten of them looked up from their computer screens the instant I tiptoed through the door.

I didn't recognise anyone, not even the teacher, snoozing peacefully beneath *The Guardian*. I was wondering whether I should pretend to read a book or something when a half-familiar voice made me swing round in horror.

'Hello, Sam.'

That was all I needed. Stephen Allbright was standing in front of me, *Great Modern Chess Openings* in one hand, egg sandwich in the other.

'All right, Dimbo?'

'No one calls me that down here. It's Stephen, or Steve if you like, it's up to you.'

'Whatever.'

'Follow me,' he said, distracted for a moment by a Year Ten girl's equations. 'I'm over in the corner, next to the periodic table.'

'No, you're all right. I think I'll just stay here.'

'Come on, Sam. I need to talk to you about your . . . predicament.'

'What predicament?'

Something about the way he rolled his eyes convinced me to follow. He took a plastic container from the top of his monitor and waved it in my face. 'Egg sandwich?'

I hardly ever talked to him on the outside, but just for a second I was tempted. 'Er, no thanks.'

'I know you haven't been to the canteen. So don't tell me you're not hungry.'

'How did you . . . ?'

'Because I've been there, Sam; got the overpriced pencil and rubber from the gift shop. Go on, take it.'

I bit gratefully into the granary triangle. 'What do you mean, you've been there?'

'You may not remember this, Sam, but I've been on the receiving end of that lot in the not so distant past. There I was, just a regular kid, like you; not popular or anything . . .'

'Thanks.'

'But someone you wouldn't mind sharing a sandwich with, someone you'd happily sit next to on the bus. And then we had that maths lesson, do you remember?'

'Er . . . no, not really.'

'I was stupid,' he said, taking his face in his hands like that painting, *The Scream*. 'I told Mrs Mendoza I could do all the algebra problems in my head. And suddenly I was different. Suddenly everyone started calling me Dimbo. Suddenly no one wanted to know me any more. Even my so called friends deserted me; just like your mate Alex.'

If only I'd been as convinced as I was trying to sound. 'Alex has *not* deserted me.'

'That's the way it looks from where I'm standing.'

'He's got . . .' (I searched for that phrase Mum was always using.) '". . . family issues", that's all.'

'You mean he's scared that if he keeps hanging out with you, this Emperor, or whatever his name is, will start making his life a misery too.'

'Alex is my best friend, he's not like that.'

'It has been known for best friends to fall out, you know.'

He was getting on my nerves now. 'Look, just leave it, OK?' I said, reaching into my rucksack for a random text-book. 'I'm trying to do my homework.'

'I've seen his crude but effective website, Samuel. And believe me, if you don't do something about it soon, things could get *extremely* unpleasant.'

'What can I do?'

'You've got to find out who this Emperor is. I could help if you like.'

'No thanks, I'll do it myself.'

'Don't make me laugh. You haven't got the faintest idea about detective work.'

The fact that he was so obviously right made him even more annoying. 'Do you mind, I'm trying to read?'

'I mean it, Sam, I want to help.'

'Shut up, Dimbo, I'm not interested, OK?'

'All right.' He shrugged, reaching for the mouse. 'But if you change your mind, you know where to find me.'

I should have bitten his hand off. Dimbo's prophecy was as accurate as his chemistry homework; something extremely unpleasant was about to happen. But I don't think even the class genius could have predicted that it involved yours truly being immortalised on film.

3.36 p.m.

'Oi, Chickenboy,' someone shouted, as I stepped out from behind the bushes at the last minute, shot up the steps and flashed my bus pass. 'What's on your iPod then?'

A sea of grinning faces swirled round towards me, and I thought I was going to puke. Eyes fixed to the floor, I shuffled down the aisle to my usual place.

Alex was in the window seat. He jumped up the moment I sat down next to him. "'Scuse me.'

'What's the matter, Lex, forgotten something?'

'Can you get out of my way please?'

'What?'

'I said, get out of my way.'

'What's the matter with . . . ?'

Everyone cheered as he pushed past me and found an empty seat further back. I reached instinctively for the front pocket of my rucksack, realising just in the nick of time that getting out my iPod was probably the worst thing I could do.

Barry the Bus Driver stamped on the accelerator and we screeched out into the afternoon traffic.

Halfway to town, my phone went off. I tried to ignore it, but it was *Mission: Impossible* to ignore a ring-tone like that. And then I noticed that a load of other phones seemed to be ringing too – a weird cacophony of 'Jingle Bells', '*Phone, am I bovvered?*', 50 Cent, '*Message, message, message, message!*' and the Monty Python theme all competed for attention.

'Oi, Chickenboy,' came a voice from the back. 'Aren't you going to answer it?'

Silence broke out the moment my thumb made contact with the keypad. Glancing back, I could see a whole bunch of Year Eights staring into their mobiles. Even a couple that hadn't got mobiles (the kid from that religious sect and the boy whose parents wouldn't even let him in the same room as a television) were watching eagerly over their shoulders.

It was the last thing I needed – someone had video-messaged me. Alex often sent clips of stuff, like him and his sister doing the dance off *The Office* or his dad's new girlfriends being stupid, but I had a pretty good idea that this would be no laughing matter.

I was spot on. Even though the picture quality reminded me of those anti-video-pirating adverts they show before movies, there was no mistaking the figure in the foreground, chomping on a cheese and tomato panini – it was me!

'Bullseye!' shouted a voice from the back of the bus, as the panini-chomper got splatted by a flying sachet of tomato ketchup. 'Got him right in the face.'

That's when I started realising that half the kids on the bus were watching it too. My suspicions were confirmed when the panini-chomper started dabbing his chops with his school tie and a great roar of laughter almost blew the roof off.

'What does Chickenboy want for Christmas?' shouted Callum Corcoran. 'Some mates, because he certainly hasn't got any.'

They brayed hysterically, like the studio audience of *Friends*.

I buried the Dad Phone deep in my rucksack, folded my arms tightly across my chest and prayed that no one could see I was quivering like Mum's natural-yoghurt maker.

'What's the matter, Chickenboy?' called Pete Hughes. 'Not *in the mood*, eh? Why don't we cheer him up with a bit of Glenn Miller?'

At first it was only a half-hearted duet, like when your parents try to get your mates to sing you 'Happy Birthday', but one by one they joined in (even Callum Corcoran, who thought singing was for girls) until the whole pack of them was roaring like a football crowd, '*Da da da da da da da da da da da da . . .*'.

I closed my eyes and tried to pretend it wasn't happening, drawing blood from my bottom lip in an ongoing battle not to be 'the boy who cried'. But my heart stopped dead in its tracks when someone slipped into the seat next to me and tapped softly on my shoulder. I tightened my stomach muscles and prepared for The Emperor to declare himself.

3.43 p.m.
'You all right, Sam?'

'What the . . . ?' Relief swiftly turned to anger when I saw that it was Stephen Allbright.

'Listen to them. What a bunch of buffoons. Everyone knows Glenn Miller didn't write 'In the Mood'.'

'Eh?'

'No,' he said, shielding himself from the cascade of crisp packets, apple cores and terms of abuse that were raining down on us from the back of the bus. 'It was a little-known trumpeter by the name of Wingy Malone. I thought that was common knowledge.'

'How about that?' came the voice from the back.

'Chickenboy and Dimbo are best buddies. Talk about the dream team.'

'Clear off, Dimbo,' I hissed, not knowing whether to admire his courage or marvel at his stupidity. 'You're only making it worse.'

'I thought you could do with a friend.'

'Look, you're not my friend, OK?'

'Right now, I reckon you could do with all the friends you can get.'

'*Please*, just go.'

But he wouldn't give up. His piercing blue eyes seemed to read me like a book.

'I can help you, Sam. All you've got to do is say the word.'

'I don't need your help.' There was only one thing for it. I kicked his shiny briefcase out of the way and fought my way down the aisle. 'Stop the bus, I want to get off.'

'But you don't get off for another two stops,' said Barry the Bus Driver.

'I promised I'd get something for my granddad.'

'Oh come on, old son. They'll soon get bored, you know.'

'Please, I need to get out.'

'Suit yourself,' said Barry the Bus Driver, pulling into a layby and opening the doors. 'But you shouldn't let them get to you, Sam. They're only having a laugh.'

'Why did the Chickenboy cross the road?' called a voice from the back.

I was down those steps so fast that I didn't even hear the punchline. I looked up at the faces in the window – Callum Corcoran shouting what could only be obscenities, Animal making gestures to the same effect, Pete Hughes smiling coolly, and I realised that I still didn't have a clue who The Emperor was.

But just when it felt like everyone was against me, I spotted a solitary, sympathetic face. Abby looked almost as upset as I was when she looked up from her paperback and gave me an encouraging smile. For the second time in as many minutes, my heart stopped dead in its tracks, only this time in a good way. Granddad was right – when the chips are down, you really do find out who your friends are.

4.18 p.m.
Granddad's room was at the end of a dingy corridor, next to the emergency exit. He once told me that the sight of 'Two-and-twenty toothless wrinklies pushing their Zimmers to the car park for a fire practice' was one of the funniest things he'd ever seen. Then again, he always did have a strange sense of humour.

I was trying to put on my happy face for him, when out of the gloom I heard someone singing. Although I couldn't make out the words, it was one of the saddest songs I'd ever heard. And the voice was so beautiful (deep and dark and velvety) that I couldn't help walking towards it. Seconds later I was standing in front of a familiar door.

I pushed it open and stepped inside. 'Hi, Granddad, what's the —?'

'Hello, Sam,' said Petal, looking embarrassed. 'Come to see your granddad, have you?'

'You know I have,' I said, feeling like I'd walked in on a scene that I didn't fully understand. 'What's happening?'

Granddad was sitting by the window in his stripy pyjamas, wiping his eyes with a spotted handkerchief. His voice was high-pitched and wheezier than usual. 'Petal and I had a bit of business to attend to. Isn't that right, m'dear?'

'That's right,' she sniffed, taking Granddad's hand and giving it a squeeze. 'Now, why I don't I leave you boys to get on with it?'

'Thank you, Petal,' he said, as she waddled out of the door. 'If you do it like that it will be absolutely splendid.'

'What's the matter with her, Granddad? Why was she crying?'

'She wasn't crying, m'boy – she was laughing.' He glanced anxiously around his tiny room, as if there were spies under the bed or something. 'Well, have you got it?'

'Yes, Granddad.'

'Good lad. You'll have to open it, I'm afraid. The old arthritis is playing me up something rotten.'

I slipped it out of the wrapper and into his clawlike hand. He held it to his nose, just like I'd seen Dad doing with a glass of wine, and then took an enormous bite. It didn't take him long to polish off the whole Mars Bar. My stomach suddenly remembered that it had only had a piece of toast and half an egg sandwich all day.

'You looked like you enjoyed that, Granddad.'

'That's because it was my last one,' he said, licking his lips. 'Not nearly as exciting as the first time of course, but then what is?'

'You going on a diet, Granddad?'

He shook his head. 'My plane's on the runway, Sam, not long to go now.'

'But you look fine,' I said, remembering what Mum had told me about white lies sometimes being kinder than the truth. 'Why do you think you're going to . . . ?'

'Let's just say I've had the call and say no more about it. But I can't get on that plane until you've heard my confession. Have you read it yet?'

'Sorry, Granddad, it's been so . . . busy at school. I've only read the bit on the train.'

'Ah yes,' he said, picking a morsel of Mars Bar out of his teeth. 'Old Tommy really saved my bacon, didn't he?'

'And you became best friends, right?'

Granddad nodded. 'It was like that in the war. You didn't fart about with formalities because you knew that any day soon one of you might cop it. It's funny though, considering how quickly we palled up, Tommy and I didn't have a lot in common.'

'What do you mean?'

'My dad was a painter and decorator and Mum took in washing. Tommy's parents owned a sweet shop. And he was a grammar-school boy, worked in a solicitor's office, whereas I left school at fourteen to go on the railways. That's why I enrolled at night school after the war.'

'So what *did* you have in common?'

'Well, we were both potty about Duke Ellington for a start. And then there was confectionery of course.' Granddad's face erupted into an enormous smile. 'What

75

with parents in the trade, so to speak, Tommy certainly knew his liquorice sticks from his sherbet lemons.'

I couldn't help remembering how Alex and me had bonded over the *Star Wars* Lego.

'But it was much more than that. We were just so comfortable in each other's company, almost like we could sense what the other one was thinking. And we knew we could rely on each other in a crisis – at least, that's what I thought.'

I couldn't help thinking about Alex again. I didn't know what Granddad was thinking about, but his smile had suddenly vanished.

'Anyway, m'boy, what's all this about it being busy at school? You've not been getting into trouble, have you?'

'Not really, Granddad, it's just . . . '

It was the perfect opportunity to tell him everything. And it ought to have been so easy. He wasn't like Dad (except physically, of course), he wouldn't have told me to pull myself together and be a man, or something. And unlike Mum, he wouldn't have wanted to relive every painful detail, in HD TV with digital surround sound. But I couldn't do it. I just couldn't bear for him to find out that his favourite grandson was a chicken.

'What's the matter, old lad? Something's bothering you, isn't it? You know what I think about secrets. Come on, Sam, why don't you tell your old granddad all about it?'

'It's nothing,' I said, trying to avoid his sad, watery eyes. 'I kind of feel a bit . . .' And that's as far as I got, because suddenly the strain of making it through a whole day without crying in public was just too much. It started somewhere deep inside me, the uncontrollable sobbing that took possession of my whole body like a mutant zombie and refused to let go.

'Come on, old chap,' said Granddad, looking faintly embarrassed and reaching creakily to ruffle my hair, 'it can't be that bad.'

'Oh yes it is, Granddad. Oh yes it is.'

Five minutes later, I was sitting on Granddad's bed, sucking a pineapple chunk from his 'secret store' and beginning to feel a bit more human.

'Right,' he said, easing himself down next to me on his two walking sticks. 'Take a deep breath and tell me all about it.'

And I still couldn't do it, but at least I could tell him part of the truth, the part I wasn't ashamed about. 'I don't want you to die, Granddad.'

'We all have to die sometime, m'boy. It's the only unavoidable fact of life.'

'What am I going to do after school?'

I realised straightaway how selfish it sounded. Granddad just smiled and offered me another pineapple chunk. 'I'm sure you'll think of something. Your dad'll be back soon anyway, but a lad like you must have plenty of pals. How about the bespectacled youth who had such fun with my wheelchair at the Christmas Bazaar? What was his name again?'

'Alex,' I mumbled, taking a pineapple chunk, keen to change the subject. 'Are you frightened, Granddad?'

At first, he opened his mouth and no sound came out.

When at last he did speak, he couldn't seem to look me in the eye. 'No, no . . . of course not.'

'I wish I was brave like you.'

'Read the rest of my story, Sam, then you'll see how brave I really am.'

'I already know how brave you are.'

'Promise me you'll do it,' he said, squeezing my hand so it hurt. 'There isn't a great deal of time, and you have to know the truth before I —'

'I promise.' I wanted to ask him if he believed in life after death and all that stuff, but it didn't seem like a very polite question for someone who was convinced he was dying. 'What shall I bring you tomorrow?'

'How about a nice tin of corned beef?'

'I'll do my best, Granddad. See you tomorrow, yeah?'

'God willing,' he said, giving me a prickly kiss on the cheek. 'Perhaps then you'll be able to tell me what's *really* bothering you.'

'Bye then,' I said, making for the door before he could ask me any more questions. 'Hope *The Weakest Link*'s good today.'

'Oh and Sam?'

'Yes.'

'I've tried to record everything just as I remember it, but when it comes to the naval part, I've had to use a bit of artistic licence.'

'What do you mean?'

'Your average sailor's language was rather colourful, to say the least, and I was no different of course. My poor old

78

hands are painful enough without having to type an obscenity every second word. So you'll just have to imagine them, I'm afraid.'

'That's OK, Granddad, I have to do exactly the same thing when I tell Mum about school.'

9.15 p.m.

'Which reminds me,' said Mum, managing to tear herself away from the TV for two seconds, 'your new girlfriend keeps calling.'

'Sure it wasn't Alex?' I said hopefully.

'No, Lexie would have said something, whereas your little lady friend just keeps hanging up on me. I tried dialling 1471, but all I get is *The caller withheld their number.*'

I didn't exactly need to be Sherlock Holmes to deduce the identity of the mystery caller. But how had The Emperor got hold of our phone number? Mum had gone ex-directory when her clients kept ringing up and swearing at her. 'Perhaps it was a wrong number.'

'What, eight times? I don't think so.' She stopped smiling and switched on her serious face. 'Tell her I'm not an ogre, Sammy. Tell her I'm actually a pretty cool mum.'

I made a mental note that if I ever got a real girlfriend I'd keep her away from Mum as long as possible. 'Yes OK, I'll do that.'

'Anyway, how was school?'

The worst thing I could have done was blab to her about The Emperor. Two seconds later she'd have frogmarched me into school demanding a meeting with Mrs Baxter, the head of Year Eight, and that would only have made things worse. The trouble was, she's a brilliant interrogator, and if I'd stuck around much longer she'd have been sure to wheedle it out of me.

'School was . . . all right. I went to the Homework Club.'

'Good for you.'

'I might go up to bed, Mum. I promised Granddad I'd read some more of his story.'

'Why don't you do it down here?'

'It's all about the war, sounds quite interesting.'

'I suppose he's been telling you how he defeated Adolf Hitler single-handedly. No wonder your father's always trying to prove what a man he is.' She slid up the sofa towards me. 'Come on, Sammy. I'll make you a hot chocolate with marshmallows in.'

See what I mean about being a brilliant interrogator?

'No, you're all right, Mum. I just want to be on my own for a bit.'

She slapped her forehead, like people do when they suddenly realise they've been stupid. 'Yes, of course you do. What am I thinking of? You don't want to be sitting down here with your old mother, do you?'

'It's not that . . .'

'I understand,' she said, sounding like a character from a terrible PSHE video. 'You're going to be wanting your privacy a lot more from now on. It's something your father really should have talked to you about, but I think I've got a book somewhere.'

'I'm sorry, Mum, I —'

'Don't be silly it's me that should . . .' Her bottom lip trembled as she waved me away. 'Off you go then, Sammy. I'll pop in and say goodnight later. But don't worry, I promise I'll knock first.'

Sliding Off
the Edge of the World

HMS RALEIGH (NAVAL TRAINING CAMP)
MAY–JUNE 1943

Tommy and I were oppos from the start. It was the kind of friendship that only happens once in a lifetime. Perhaps you haven't found a best pal yet, but believe me, Sam, you'll know when you do. We were that close we could almost read each other's minds. Me and Tommy told each other everything. (I believe I even confessed to being a little scared.) There were no secrets between us. How could there be when we knew each other so well?

And for some unknown reason, Sharky Beal took a shine to 'the Professor' and me. Provided he wasn't rabbiting on about how desperate he was to 'see some action', he could be pretty good company. So, when we weren't doubling around the parade ground or practising our bends and hitches ('You do not call them knots!'), the three of us would gather outside the NAAFI (a sort of naval canteen), with a cup of filthy coffee, to chew the fat.

But you know, Sam, Tommy did have a

82

secret. And although it pales in comparison with the whopper I've carted around for the last sixty years, it wasn't exactly the sort of thing you'd boast about to your ship-mates. On our last day at HMS Raleigh, I found out what it was.

'Right, lads,' said Tiddley Norton, a cur-mudgeonly Chief Petty Officer who'd been brought out of retirement for the duration. 'Before we let you loose on the enemy, there's one last thing we have to do.'

He marched us over to a Nissen hut on the edge of the parade ground and told us to strip off. After six weeks of naval disci-pline, we knew better than to question orders. Two minutes later, fifty bemused recruits were standing to attention in only their underpants.

''Ere, Chief,' said Sharky. 'It's another one of them medicals, isn't it? Is matron going to feel my wotsits?'

Tiddley Norton grinned sadistically. 'You'll feel my boot up your jacksie if you don't shut up, Beal. And seeing as you're such a comedian, you and your oppos can go first.'

In the middle of the hut stood a round metal tank, about ten feet in diameter and eight feet deep, with an iron ladder leading over the side into the water and a viewing platform manned by an officer with a long bamboo pole in his hand.

Tiddley Norton handed out some lifejackets and instructed us to put them on. 'God willing, it won't happen to any of you,' he said, 'but if the worst comes to the worst, like it did for my old oppo Dusty Miller at the Battle of Jutland, you'll need to have confidence in your equipment. That's what this exercise is all about.'

On Tiddley's command, each man was to get into the water and climb down the ladder to the bottom of the tank. When ('and only when') the man with the pole tapped you on the shoulder you were to let go of the ladder and float to the surface.

'Right then, Beal,' said Tiddley Norton. 'Why don't you show us all how it's done?'

As Sharky made his way to the foot of the ladder, I felt a clammy hand on my shoulder.

Tommy's voice was so brimming with terror that I hardly recognised it. 'I can't do it, Ray. They can't make me, can they?'

'What do you mean, you can't do it?'

'I can't swim,' said Tommy, his finger-nails digging deeper into my shoulder blade. 'I'm terrified of water.'

At first I thought he was joking. His

wild, staring eyes told me otherwise.

'Why did you join the navy then?'

'My dad was on the Indomitable in the last war. He practically marched me down to the recruiting office. What am I going to do, Ray?'

'You'll be fine,' I said, trying to convince myself, but not really succeeding.

Meanwhile, Sharky's head had disappeared beneath the murky water.

'I've got to get out of here,' said Tommy.

I told him that orders were orders.

'That's what I hate about this place: orders, orders and more bloody orders.'

I told him he shouldn't let it get to him.

'What, "Illegitimi nil carborundum" you mean?'

I told him I didn't know what he was talking about.

'It's pidgen Latin,' he said. 'It means, don't let the bastards grind you down.'

Sharky broke the surface of the water like a tin-fish (torpedo) and clambered out of the tank. 'All aboard for the Skylark!'

'Well done, Beal,' said Tiddley Norton grudgingly. 'Now then, Riley, seeing as you seem to have ants in your pants, you'd better go next.'

Tommy's face was as white as asbestos. 'I

can't do it, Chief.'

Tiddley's face was as red as Mr Punch. 'What did you say, lad?'

'Let me go next, Chief,' I said. 'Riley's not feeling too clever. He'll be all right in a minute.'

'Probably coming down with psychotalclapsica,' volunteered Sharky.

'All right,' said Tiddley Norton, casting a quizzical eye over Tommy's ashen features, 'but you're next, Professor, so you'd better pull yourself together.'

The tank held no terrors for me. I loved being underwater. I'd spent most of my childhood on Brighton beach, and liked nothing better than to dive down to the sea floor and time how long I could sit there. (The trick is to empty your lungs first, Sam.) It's so peaceful beneath the waves. It's one of the few places you can really hear yourself think.

And there at the bottom of the tank, I suddenly had the most terrible thought: What if Tommy didn't make it? I know it sounds selfish, but I was terrified they'd have him court-martialled for insubordination. Life without Tommy would have been unbearable, as I was soon to find out.

By the time I came up for air, all hell had

broken loose. Tiddley Norton's parade-ground holler rose above the feverish chatter of his young recruits. 'Come back here, Riley. Where the hell do you think you're going?'

The door of the hut was wide open. Tommy was nowhere to be seen.

'Riley, get back in here now!'

But it was Sharky who appeared at the door first. 'It's all right, Chief,' he said, dragging Tommy behind him. 'Riley come over a bit queer, so I had to take him outside to be ill.'

'To be what?' barked Tiddley Norton.

'Must have been that suet pudding, Chief,' said Sharky. 'But he's tickety-boo now, aren't you, Professor?'

Tommy nodded unconvincingly.

'All right, Riley, this is your last chance, lad. Get up that ladder now!'

I could hardly bear to look. Tommy's face had acquired a greenish tinge. He stood staring up at the tank, motionless but for the almost imperceptible quiver of his knees.

'Go on, Tommy,' I whispered. 'Illegitimi nil carbo whatdoyoucallit.'

He managed a sickly smile and shuffled towards the ladder like someone approaching the scaffold. At first, every rung was sheer torture. But slowly he gathered momentum until, by the time he'd reached the top, he almost looked like a real sailor.

I'd seen the terror in his eyes. It was little short of a miracle. Bravery has nothing to do with what you're frightened of, Sam. We're all afraid of something, sometimes with good reason. It's how you deal with your fear that really counts.

There was a wry smile on Tiddley Norton's face as he signalled to the man with the stick. I can't tell you how proud I was when Tommy's face appeared above the side of the tank.

Of course, had I known what was going to happen little more than a month later, I would have made him swear a solemn oath never to set foot near water again.

The next day we were ordered to Pompey Barracks (where the food was slightly more tolerable, you'll be pleased to hear) to await our first posting. Two weeks later, Tommy, Sharky Beal and I had commandeered a plot not much bigger than a postage stamp, on the vomit-strewn lower deck of the troop-ship Orion.

'Gonna see some action,' muttered Sharky. 'Gonna make my family proud.'

We'd had six weeks' training, we hadn't a clue where we were going, we hardly knew the difference between a bulkhead and a butterfly clip and most of us were barely out of short trousers, but according to the 'Ministry of Twerps', we were ready for war.

9.43 p.m.

I didn't feel like reading any more. All that stuff about Granddad and Tommy Riley being such good friends had left me really fed up. Me and Alex had been like that in the 'good old days', but now he wouldn't even sit next to me on the bus, and every time he saw me he was like, 'Get out of my face.'

I lay back on the bed, thinking that things couldn't possibly get any worse when Mum knocked on the door and proved me wrong again.

'Letter for you, Sam,' she said, handing me a brown A4 envelope, like the ones she sometimes kept her case notes in. 'It arrived just now. Someone rang the bell, but by the time I got there they'd vanished – must be from your girlfriend.'

I studied the neat, old-fashioned writing on the envelope: *For the attention of Master S Tennant.*

'Yeah, 'spect so, Mum.'

She hovered expectantly beneath my Grade Three clarinet certificate. 'Bit formal, isn't it? I thought you guys didn't believe in snail mail. And come to think of it, I wouldn't be particularly thrilled for any daughter of mine to be out delivering love letters at this time of night.' Her face softened a little. 'Still, it's very romantic, I suppose.'

'Yes, Mum.'

'Well, come on, aren't you going to open it?'

'In a minute, Mum.'

'Ah well, you can't blame a girl for trying.' She sat on the

90

edge of my bed and pulled me towards her in a sort of motherly headlock. Her hair smelled of green apples. 'Which reminds me, I need to talk to you about Thursday.'

'It's not recycling day again, is it?'

'I'm going to be working late, I'm afraid. So after you've seen your granddad, I want you to walk up to the clinic to meet me.'

I hated that CAMHS place. It was full of weirdo kids and stupid posters with totally obvious stuff on them like, *Be careful with boiling water*. 'Couldn't you do it some other day?'

'This is serious, Sam. I've had to schedule an extra session with the whole family. The panic attacks are getting worse. If we don't get to the bottom of this child's problems soon, someone could get hurt. I mean I know that wild threats are part and parcel of the whole adolescent Jekyll-and-Hyde scenario, but just occasionally one of them actually means it.'

'OK then,' I said, shaking the envelope like a Christmas present, knowing in my heart that it wasn't the latest Bond DVD. 'I'll come straight over after I've been to Granddad's.'

'Night love, sleep tight, don't let the . . .' Sometimes Mum looked at me as if I was the most precious thing in the world; it was nice, but kind of scary too. 'Enjoy your letter.'

As soon as I was certain she wasn't going to barge in again and remind me about my PE kit or something, I ripped open the envelope and slid out a single sheet of white A4.

The words jumped out at me like the knife guy in that movie Mum said I shouldn't really have been watching. I didn't want to look but, just like that movie, I couldn't help myself.

I must have read it at least ten times before I stuffed the horrible thing under my pillow and tried to figure out what to do next. I can't have been thinking straight because the first thing I wanted was some music. If the Duke couldn't help me to get my head together nobody could.

I grabbed my rucksack and rifled through the front pocket. Mum was right – it did need a 'good old clear out'. It was like a lucky dip in there: I found half a packet of Polos, a protractor, fifty cocktail umbrellas (don't ask), the tooth that came out in German, a Lego Hagrid, my lesson planner, and something soft and sticky . . . *but no iPod.*

Perhaps it had fallen out in food-tech (that couldn't be right; I was always so careful with it), or maybe I was doing what Mum called 'boys' looking', and it was right at the bottom somewhere. So I carried on rooting around for a bit, like a doctor trying to resuscitate a patient he already knew was dead. In the end the diagnosis was obvious: someone had stolen my iPod.

But how? I'd had my rucksack with me all day. And why? You have no idea how much chicken poo I'd had to clean up before Mum would let me order it. This couldn't be happening. My life was such a total disaster area, I almost wished I was de— No, no, it hadn't quite come to that yet. What was Tommy Riley's motto? *Illegitimi nil carborundum?* And what did it mean again?

There was only one thing for it. I took out the Dad Phone, already feeling slightly better in the warm glow of its illuminated keypad. Just to hear his voice would be enough. If I'd been more of a Hardman like him I wouldn't have been in this state in the first place.

'Is that you, Sam?' said Dad.

'I just called to say hi.'

'Great to hear from you son, but I'm just running through my race plan. Can I call you back afterwards? It wasn't anything urgent, was it?'

I couldn't let him hear that I was nearly crying. 'No, Dad.'

'Listen Sam, how's your granddad?' he said anxiously.

'He says he's going to . . .' (It was no good, I couldn't tell him. I knew how upset he got if he thought Granddad was unhappy.) 'He says he's going down to the lounge for the sing-song tonight.'

'Great,' said Dad, sounding mightily relieved. 'Now if you don't mind, son, I need to get on. I'll call you after the race.'

'Good luck, Dad. Oh and Dad . . . Dad? *Dad* . . .'

He'd gone. That was it then. What else could I do? No iPod, I didn't dare go on the internet in case some idiot started emailing me, and even my own father hadn't got time for a chat. There was nothing to stop me reaching under my pillow and pulling out The Emperor's letter. But I didn't need to read it again. The words were light-scribed deep into my memory bank for all eternity.

WANT TO KNOW
WHO I AM?

C U 1st BREAK
THURSDAY IN
MUSIC BLOC TOILET

THE EMPEROR

THURSDAY
(WEEK TWO)

10.57 a.m.

The phoney war was nearly over. In a funny sort of way, I was relieved. Even though I'd stopped catching the bus and done everything in my power to keep a low profile, hidden menace lurked everywhere and I had a horrible feeling it could all kick off at any second.

On Tuesday lunchtime, they'd pinned a photograph of my infants' school nativity play to the noticeboard. Actually I was supposed to be a camel, but underneath, someone had scrawled *Kentucky Fried Chickenboy* in big red letters. On Wednesday, I was so spooked by their whispered threats and chicken noises that Mrs Mendoza gave me my first ever detention for 'persistent inattention in class'.

They were the loneliest forty-eight hours of my life. Mum was too wrapped up in her work to notice I was constantly on the verge of tears, Dad obviously didn't have time to return my calls, and Granddad kept insisting he was 'not long for this world'. By Thursday morning, I was a bleary-eyed wreck.

The bell for first break felt like a death knell. There were a million and one things I'd rather be doing, but something told me I'd have to go through with it.

'Betcha can't wait till tomorrow, eh, Chickenboy?' said Callum Corcoran.

And his words were still ringing in my ears as I slipped out of the IT suite and made my way across the courtyard, scanning the home economics block for hidden assassins, praying that I wasn't being followed.

Callum was right of course, Friday couldn't come soon enough, but I had a nasty feeling he was talking about the *HMS Belfast* trip and not that glorious moment when the last bell went and school was over for another week.

I crouched behind one of the new wastepaper bins that no one used (there was a special section for recycling cans) and waited for the rest of my 'classmates' to pass by on their way to the canteen. They looked so happy, laughing and joking and doing that thing where you slap another kid's head and shout 'spam'. Ever since The Emperor arrived on the scene, feuds that had festered since primary school seemed to have gone out of the window. Chelsea was showing Gaz Lulham her new mobile, Pete Hughes and Animal were discussing that website where they randomly microwave stuff, and suddenly Callum Corcoran was everybody's best mate. Even Dimbo lumbered along happily, squinting in the late-morning sun and munching an egg sandwich.

As soon as they were out of earshot, I scuttled over to the medical suite, taking the shadowy route beneath the covered walkway until I was standing in front of the music block. And that's when I started having second thoughts. I approached the automatic doors like a bomb-disposal guy inching towards an abandoned rucksack. If it wasn't for something Granddad had said, I wouldn't have been there. *'It's how you deal with fear that really counts.'* It was my chance to prove him right. I was going to confront my nemesis. It was time to meet The Emperor face to face.

But supposing it was a trap? Supposing they were all hiding in the cubicles? Supposing it was an ambush and they were going to beat me up? I swallowed down a mouthful of vomit and looked up at the menacing skies. I could just hear Mum breaking into one of her global warming medleys. When I looked down again, the music-block doors were sliding open. As the first drops of rain started drumming on the covered walkway, I reached into my jacket pocket for the blob of Blu-Tack I sometimes used as a worry ball, and stepped inside.

I ran up the concrete staircase, but the bleak fluorescence of the music-block corridor soon took the spring out of my step, and I made my way towards the boys' toilets like an over-cautious snail. For the first time, I clocked that Miss Hoolyhan had plastered the walls with stuff about 'the great composers'. I was just reading that *Russian genius Dimitri Shostakovich (1906-1975) was also a qualified football referee*, when I'm sure I heard a stifled laugh.

'What's that? Who's there?'

There were no music rehearsals first break on Thursdays. Apart from someone torturing a cello somewhere, there didn't seem to be anyone else about, but by now the mocking laughter was so overpowering it felt like it was inside my head. By the time I realised it was coming from the speakers above me, there was also a thunderous drum track (like the stuff Callum Corcoran gave Miss Hoolyhan when she let us bring in our own CDs) and an echoey chorus of the saxophone part from 'In The Mood'.

'Shut up, shuuuut up!' I screamed. But it only got worse: on top of the mix was the unmistakable sound of Mum's telephone voice going, *'Who is this please? Who is this please? Who is this please?'* on a continuous loop.

'Stop it, stop it . . .' I charged down the music-block corridor, like a two-hundred-metre runner pumped with steroids. All I wanted was to get that throbbing soundtrack out of my head. Five minutes before, my only emotion had been fear, but as soon as The Emperor started playing mind games involving my mum, it was more like seventy per cent fear and thirty per cent anger. I dived for the finishing line, bursting into the boys' toilets and skidding to a halt in front of the urinals.

'OK then,' I said, surprised at how steady my voice sounded. 'I'm here now. What do you want?'

And then someone killed the 'music'.

After the ear-splitting silence that followed, I didn't sound quite so confident. 'Look, I don't know who you are, but why don't you tell me what's bothering you and maybe . . .'

And then the lights went out.

The last dollop of anger drained from my fingertips and I cowered in the darkness, arms raised in front of my face like a boxer on the ropes. '*Please* . . . Look, just tell what I'm supposed to have done . . . I didn't mean to . . . If you don't like me I can always change . . . Please, please, it's really dark in here . . . '

The solo game of Blind Man's Buff continued for what seemed like an eternity until, as if in answer to my feverish prayers, the light flickered on again, and two seconds later I heard stifled giggles outside the door followed by the sound of galloping feet in the corridor.

I dashed outside, but it was too late. All I saw was the back of two school jackets disappearing into the stairwell. So much for facing my fears – I was drenched with sweat, my left eyeball wouldn't stop quivering and I still didn't have a clue who The Emperor was.

'Are you all right, Samuel?'

'*What* . . . You made me jump, Miss.'

Miss Hoolyhan was wearing some music department headphones round her neck. 'Sorry about that.'

'Did you see who they were, Miss?'

'I haven't seen a soul,' she said. 'I thought everyone was out on the field.'

'But you must have heard that terrible noise.'

'I've been doing my relaxation CD. Dead to the world, I'm afraid. Look, are you sure you're all right, Sam? Your eyes look terribly —'

'Hay fever, Miss.'

'Listen, Sam, if there's anything you want to talk about, I'm always here you know.'

I was *that* close to telling her. 'I'm fine, Miss.'

'Well all right then,' she said reluctantly. 'But before you go outside, I think you'd better pop into the loo and freshen up.'

'Yes, Miss. Thanks, Miss.'

Perhaps Granddad and I had more in common than I thought. The first thing I did was fill the sink right to the top and dunk my head in it; funny how that always seemed to calm me down. But it didn't last. After a minute or so (my record was sixty-eight seconds), I had to come up for air, and that's when I saw the writing on the mirror.

There in blood red, just like The Emperor's letter and the picture on the noticeboard, was the word: *SUCKER*.

I stared at it for a moment. Dad was always saying I should never let my emotions get the better of me, but something inside was about to snap.

11.13 a.m.

I burst out of the music block toilets and hit the ground running; along the corridor, down the stairs, out into the bucketing rain and across the courtyard, more furious with every soggy step, so that by the time I got to the canteen I was feeling about one per cent fear and ninety-nine per cent blind rage.

And there they all were – snouts deep in polystyrene cartons of pasta, stuffing their faces with Hula Hoops and washing it down with Capri Sun. A ripple of laughter passed around the canteen when they saw my half-drenched figure in the doorway.

'Look,' said Callum Corcoran. 'Chickenboy's wet himself.'

But I was so angry I didn't even care. There was a stunned silence as I marched up to them and demanded, 'Which one of you is it then? Don't just sit there giggling like schoolgirls.'

'Don't you like girls or something?' said Pete Hughes.

I squeezed harder on my blob of Blu-Tack and moved in for the kill. 'Come on, I want to know. What's the matter, you a bloody coward or something?'

The usual high-pitched 'Oooh' went up.

But I stood my ground. 'I'm not leaving until I find out who you are. I mean it – so come on, which one of you is The Emperor?'

And it felt good, taking control for once. I sensed their panic. The nervous coughing and furtive glances which followed could mean only one thing: The Emperor was about to reveal himself.

There were quite a lot of things that irritated my dad, but one thing that *really* bugged him were those two-hour detective shows on ITV when it turned out that the one who'd 'done it' was an obscure relative of the victim, who hadn't even appeared until the last five minutes. But this was real life, so I suppose I shouldn't have been too surprised when it turned out to be the first person I'd thought of.

Callum Corcoran rose slowly, took a couple of steps towards me and grinned. 'I'm The Emperor,' he said.

It was completely illogical, but just knowing who hated me so much was such a relief.

But then Gaz Lulham stood up too. 'I'm The Emperor,' he said.

Followed by Chelsea: '*I'm* The Emperor.'

And Animal: 'I'm The Emperor.'

And Pete Hughes: 'I'm The Emperor.'

And a random selection of various other Year Eight jokers, until my head was exploding with their brutal laughter and I stumbled into the sheeting rain, running blindly until I came to the only place in the school where I knew I could be alone.

11.15 a.m.

The Millennium Pagoda was described in the school prospectus as 'a purpose-built relaxation area for your child to chill out.' So of course, no one went there. It didn't help that it was halfway to the all-weather hockey pitches and looked like something out of a Pokémon movie.

Rain raced down the ornamental roof, forming a watery wall of death as it splattered onto the concrete below. I sat on the grey, wooden picnic bench with my head in my hands, shivering, confused, wondering if the nightmare would ever end.

All the fight had gone out of me. I didn't even care if they saw me crying. Nothing made sense any more. For the first time in my life, I almost wished I was dead.

'Sam, Sam, is that you?'

A red cagoule appeared out of the deluge. I recognised it instantly – it was the one that Pete Hughes had said looked like 'a pregnant Father Christmas' on the Year Seven field trip. It stepped into the Millennium Pagoda and sat down opposite me.

'Are you OK, Sam? You look really tired.'

'I'm fine, just a bit of . . . hay fever. And I haven't been sleeping too well.'

Abby pulled back her hood. A shock of mousey hair tumbled onto her shoulders. 'I saw what they did to you. Here, have another tissue.'

'Thanks. This is getting to be a bit of a habit, isn't it?'

When she smiled, I didn't even notice the brace. All I saw were her sad brown eyes. 'I know what it feels like, Sam. Hurts, doesn't it?'

'Yeah.'

Her soft, comforting voice was like one of those massage chairs they have in shopping malls. 'We could talk, if it helps.'

'I'm not sure if . . .'

'I won't tell anyone,' she said, taking a small box from the front pouch of her cagoule. 'I can keep a secret, you know.'

'It's not that.'

She offered me the box. 'Here, have one of these. And then you can tell me all about it.'

'What are they?'

'Turkish delight – my mum's "fiancé" brought them back from his business trip.'

'Thanks.' It was soft and sticky and a little bit sickly, but it

103

hit the spot. 'Your mum's getting married – isn't that a bit weird?'

'Tell me about it.'

'You don't sound too pleased.'

'There's not a lot I can do about it, is there?'

She drummed on the tabletop with her delicate fingers. I got this silly urge to reach across and take her hand. Luckily I didn't go through with it. 'I like your nails.'

'Never mind that, Sam, why don't you tell me exactly what's been happening?'

So I went right back to the beginning and told her everything, starting with my cyber-murder, right through to the final humiliation in the music block toilets and that unfortunate incident in the canteen. And I mean *everything*; Abby was such a good listener that I even threw in the bit about Mum and my imaginary girlfriend. She didn't interrupt, just smiled in the bits where I tried to make it sound funnier than it really was and let me keep rabbiting on until the bitter end.

'That's awful, Sam. No wonder you feel so bad about yourself.'

'It's OK. Talking to you has actually made things a lot better. It's really helped – thanks.'

The hint of a blush slid slowly down her face, like the final curtain. 'That's brilliant Sam, but . . .' Her voice trailed off. She sucked in her cheeks to form two perfect dimples.

'But what?'

'It's probably nothing.'

'Come on, it's not like my life can get any worse.'

'Well,' said Abby licking her lips, 'did you see that horrible Chickenboyz website last night?'

'Right now, I don't ever want to go online again.'

'I thought I might be able to work out who The Emperor was, but while I was on there I read something about the trip tomorrow.'

I'd been trying to forget about it. A sharp shiver fizzed up my backbone.

'What did it say?'

'Doesn't matter.'

'Come on, Abby, what did it say?'

She slipped a cherry-red fingernail into her mouth and chewed nervously. 'It's probably nothing.'

'Please, you've got to tell me.'

'Well, it said . . . ' She shook her head and hugged herself so tightly that her cagoule look like a straightjacket. 'It said The Emperor was going to . . . kill you.'

'It said *what*?'

'You know what kids are like?' she said, squeezing out of the picnic table. 'They make out they're going to do stuff, but they never go through with it.'

'That's exactly what my mum says.'

'Does she now.'

'What am I going to do, Abby?'

She backed towards the curtain of rain. 'I shouldn't have said anything. I didn't want to scare you even more. I just thought you ought to know.'

'I'm glad you told me.'

'Look, I have to go. My trousers are soaking. If I don't

change out of them before my clarinet lesson it'll bring on my asthma. You will be careful, won't you, Sam? I'd hate for you to get hurt.'

'Thanks.'

'I'll be thinking about you.'

And then something magical happened. I wasn't sure why, but somehow, just talking to Abby had made me stronger. She was about to brave the storm when an extraordinary idea popped into my head. I couldn't believe I was about to say it. 'Abby?'

'Yes.'

'Would you like to go out with me sometime?'

She looked almost as surprised as I was. Her face erupted like an angry volcano and within nanoseconds it was almost indistinguishable from her cagoule. 'Well, I . . .'

'There's that new LaserQuest at the leisure centre, or we could go to a movie or something.'

I felt like a contestant on a talent show during that ago-nising silence before the judges tell you if you're going to boot camp. I can't tell you how relieved I was when her look of sheer astonishment rearranged itself into a broad smile.

'Why not? Might be fun.'

'Is that a yes then?'

'It's a maybe, Sam. Let's wait until . . .' She waved, pulled on her hood and stepped haltingly into the rain.

I watched until she was just a tiny red blob in the distance, but I was so pleased with myself that, even before she'd got to the sports hall, I was itching to text Alex. It was only after I'd reached for my mobile that I realised just how futile it would be. It took two seconds for the old feelings of hopelessness to resurface.

But this time there was a huge difference. Ten minutes ago, I'd wanted to die; now what I really wanted was my old life back. Ten minutes ago, I'd been ready to lie down and surrender. Having a friend like Abby had given me the courage to stand up and fight.

I hadn't a clue how I was going to do it. I was so petrified I could hardly breathe. The last time I'd got into a scrap was in the nursery sandpit – come to that I didn't even know who I was fighting against – but I was ready for war.

What I needed now was a powerful ally. There was only person who could help me. I only hoped I hadn't left it too late.

1.35 p.m.

'It's quite simple, Suzy. If x equals minus four, then the first factor will be zero. And if x equals two, the *second* factor will be zero. But – and this is crucial – if *any* factor is zero, then the entire product will be zero. OK?'

'Thanks, Stephen. You explain it loads better than old Mendozey.'

Dimbo beamed at his Year Ten protégé. His smile did a runner the moment he saw me. 'What do *you* want?'

'Can I have a quick word please?'

'Can't you see that I'm busy?'

'Please. Look I need your help, it's urgent.'

'Oh, you need my help now, do you? I thought you'd

made it abundantly clear that my overtures of friendship were entirely unwanted.'

'Please. I'm desperate.'

He sized me up like an equation. 'All right, you'd better follow me . . . Any more questions, Suzy, just give me a shout.'

He led me over to the periodic table, took a Dairylea Dunker from behind his monitor and gestured me to sit down. 'OK, Sam, what's the problem?'

I handed him The Emperor's letter. 'Someone put this through our door on Monday night.'

He held it up to the light, sniffed at it like our neighbours' fox terrier and snorted dismissively. 'Bit melodramatic, don't you think?'

'Is it?'

His notebook was covered in hieroglyphics. He turned to a clean page and clicked the top of his ballpoint. 'I think you'd better start talking.'

So I went right back to the beginning and told him everything, starting with my cyber-murder, right through to the final humiliation in the music block toilets and that unfortunate incident in the canteen – although this time I left out the bit about Mum and my imaginary girlfriend. Dimbo was such an impatient listener. Every five seconds, he asked me another totally irrelevant question – 'Who's your broadband provider?' 'Miss Hoolyhan was wearing head-phones, you say?' – and scribbled in his notebook. By the time I'd finished, I was starting to wonder if it was such a good idea.

Dimbo just looked bored. 'Is that it?'

'What?'

'You said it was urgent.'

It felt like bad luck even to mention it. 'There's one more thing. It's about the trip tomorrow.'

'Oh yes.'

I whispered it into the palm of my hand. 'The Emperor says he's going to kill me.'

'Does he now?'

'Abby told me. She saw it on that website.'

'Who, Brace Face, you mean?'

'Don't call her that, she's really nice.'

He shrugged and mopped up his last morsel of Dairylea. 'She's a reasonably proficient clarinettist I suppose.'

'Come on, Stephen, you've got to help me. What am I going to do?'

'You can start by not panicking.'

'That's all very well for you.'

'Oh, so you don't remember Dead Dimbo Day then? "Kill Dimbo and raise money for Comic Relief." I suppose you laughed as loudly as the rest of them.'

'Well . . . '

'I had to put up with threats every day, Sam, and most of the time that's exactly what they are – just threats. You know what prepubescents are like.'

'That's what my mum says.'

'Yes, I know.' Dimbo twitched anxiously.

'*What* did you say?'

It wasn't half as explosive as Abby's, but I felt sure he was blushing. 'Nothing, I —'

'How do you know my mum?'

He glanced surreptitiously around Club Nerd. 'We met professionally . . . last Christmas.'

'What about all that confidentiality stuff? How did you know she was my mum?'

'Apart from the fact she's called Dr Tennant, you mean?' said Dimbo witheringly. 'Little Harry Potter on her desk was a bit of a giveaway.'

'But how . . . I mean why . . . What were you . . . ?'

'Remember that time I was off school for a month?'

'Not really.'

'I didn't want to go back. Your mum showed me that being different wasn't necessarily such a bad thing. She also taught me a couple of coping strategies. That's why I'm going to help you.'

'But how?'

'We can start by examining the evidence.'

We slipped unnoticed into the music block and I took him on a guided tour. 'There's the speaker. I thought they were all wired up to the office.'

'Wouldn't be too difficult to override,' said Dimbo, squinting down towards the store cupboard. 'Once he'd done that he could operate his audio device from virtually anywhere. But he'd need someone to tip him the wink, so I'd say we're definitely dealing with two of them.'

'I've already told you about Ollyg78.'

'That could just have been a cover. Now let's have a look in here.'

My heart picked up speed as I pushed open the door and sniffed the air freshener. It was exactly as I'd left it – washbasin still half full and *SUCKER* inscribed on the mirror in big red letters. 'What are you doing?'

'Just checking,' said Dimbo, running his finger over the *K* and sniffing it. 'That's interesting.'

'What about when the lights went out? How did they do that?'

Dimbo rolled his eyes and turned his attention to the contents of the wastepaper bin. 'The switch in the corridor, perhaps?'

'Oh yeah.'

He continued for another ten minutes, crawling under the washbasins, scribbling notes and taking pictures with his mobile. 'Right, that's it,' he said at last. 'I've got everything I want.'

We walked in silence to the stairs. Dimbo was deep in thought. I didn't want to interrupt him, but in the end I couldn't help myself.

'So who is it then? You've got to tell me – who's The Emperor?'

'I haven't the faintest idea.'

'What?'

'This isn't a silly TV show, Sam.'

'Then what were you doing back there?'

'Building a profile.'

'What's the use of a stupid profile? It's the *HMS Belfast* trip tomorrow and we don't even know who it is.'

We stepped into the natural light. Callum Corcoran and

111

Animal were up to their ankles in the huge puddle that had formed after the morning's downpour, kicking water at each other.

Dimbo made instinctively for the shadows. 'Cheer up,' he said, as we came to a halt outside our tutor base. 'We may not know who The Emperor is yet, but the profiling has made one thing abundantly clear.'

'What exactly?'

'Now we know you can't take these threats too lightly.'

'What are you saying?'

'I'm saying we're not dealing with your average St Thomas's idiot here. I'm saying this Emperor is fairly intelligent, clearly a risk taker, not to mention dangerously unpredictable. I'm saying you've got to be careful, Sam.'

A whole crowd of them pushed past us on their way to registration. As they piled into the classroom, someone whispered, 'Hope you're not scared of water, Chickenboy.'

'Did you hear that?'

Dimbo nodded grimly.

'What am I going to do?'

'I've told you. You've got to get to The Emperor before The Emperor gets to you. There's nothing more frightening than the unknown, Samuel. But crack The Emperor's identity and we're laughing.'

'You just said you hadn't a clue who he was.'

'I'm working on it.'

'But what about the *Belfast* trip?'

'When you're on the train, you'll have to do what I did when we went to the Natural History Museum.'

'Eh?'

'Sneak up into First Class. No one will bother you there. I'll text you if the ticket collector's coming. Slip your number into my briefcase when no one's looking.'

'How about when we're on the boat itself?'

'Stick as close to Miss Stanley and "I'll do the funnies" as possible.'

'What if I lose them?'

'I'll be right behind you. The minute I see something fishy, I'll let you know.'

The thought of Dimbo as some sort of personal bodyguard didn't inspire much confidence. 'It will be all right, won't it, Stephen?'

Dimbo glanced into our tutor base. A re-enactment of the Battle of the Somme seemed to have broken out. 'You could just bunk off for the day.'

My eyes were drawn to the courageous figure in No Man's Land. Water bombs were exploding all around her, but Abby sat at her desk, quietly reading her latest paperback. And it was at that moment that I realised why it was so important to stand up to The Emperor. It wasn't just for myself, but for Abby and Dimbo and all the other kids who dreaded going to school because someone was giving them a tough time. Maybe I could give Granddad something to be proud of after all.

'No,' I said, 'I have to go through with it. If I don't do something now, it might go on for years.'

Dimbo nodded. 'That's either very brave, or incredibly stupid.'

4.07 p.m.

'Now you mustn't be frightened, Sam. Your granddad might be a bit confused, but the doctor's been up and she says he's not in any pain.'

'He was fine yesterday.'

Petal was balancing a tray of half-empty coffee cups and broken biscuits. 'Life's like that, I'm afraid. One moment you're bouncing along full of beans, and five minutes later . . .'

'He *said* he was going to die.'

'I've seen that a few times,' said Petal. 'It's like they know.'

'I don't want him to . . .'

'Of course you don't,' said Petal, trying hard to smile. 'Now, why don't you have a nice biscuit and then pop up and see him? I'll come with you if you like.'

I bit into a stale Rich Tea finger. 'It's OK. I'm not frightened.'

Down in the residents' lounge, an organist in a sparkly suit was leading a sing-song. Granddad had once told me that he'd cut his throat if he had to sit through another chorus of 'Roll Out the Barrel'. That's why I was half smiling when I reached the end of the corridor and tapped on his door. 'Granddad . . . Granddad, it's me.'

I tried again, but there was still no answer, so I took a deep breath and stepped into the rancid gloom. 'Sorry I'm late. I missed the bus again. Look, what's happening? Granddad, are you OK?'

It was as black as night and someone had gone psycho

with the air-freshener. All I could hear was the distant moan of 'It's a Long Way to Tipperary' and the agonised wail of Granddad's breathing.

'It's me, Sam.'

Still no answer. I didn't like to wake him, but I didn't fancy sitting in the twilight zone for half an hour either. I tiptoed to the window and opened a chink in the curtains. The sun slashed the darkness like a lightsaber.

'DON'T OPEN THE CURTAINS!' screamed a high-pitched voice. A moment later, his bedside lamp clicked on and I saw Granddad sitting bolt upright in bed with a crazed expression on his face.

'What's the matter, Granddad?'

'Don't open the curtains. I'm not ready yet.'

'What do you want to sit in the dark for?' I said, sounding just like Mum when I closed the blinds so I could see the Xbox properly. 'I think the sun's coming out again.'

'Can you see anyone?' whispered Granddad.

'What are you talking about?'

'Down on the bench; have a look for me, there's a good lad.'

Two emos were kissing. Every time the girl came up for air, she took a swig of Diet Coke. 'There's no one, Granddad, just a couple of teenagers.'

'Thank the Lord for that.'

He looked about a hundred years old, and a million miles away from the jolly old man who used to give me piggyback rides round the garden and let me nail old bits of wood together in his shed. I hated it when he got all crazy like that.

'I've got that sherbet fountain you asked for, Granddad.'

He fell back onto his mountain of pillows and let out a muffled groan. 'Thank you, m'boy. But you'll have to help me, I'm afraid.'

I bit the top off the liquorice and held it to his lips. 'There you go.'

He took a couple of sucks and then stopped to catch his breath. 'Well, that takes me back.'

'Don't you want any more?'

'You finish it, m'boy. I've had enough.'

'What shall I bring tomorrow?'

He shook his head. 'I don't think you need worry about that.'

'But Granddad . . .'

He stretched out a trembling hand and ruffled my hair. 'I've never been the sort of chap to wear his heart on his sleeve. God knows, it drove your grandmother barmy. The point is . . . life would be pretty pointless without other people – important people that is. And when I say important, I mean, well, the people we . . . love. What I'm trying to say, Sam, is that it's been a real pleasure getting to know you. I've been so proud to have such a, well, such a wonderful grandson. I'm really very . . . fond of you, you know. And I just wanted to tell you that . . .'

'I love you too, Granddad.'

'Yes, well . . . that's good then.' He looked almost as relieved as I was when Mum told me I didn't have to be a pageboy at Auntie Lucy's wedding. 'Now, have you read it yet?'

I'd been carrying it round in my rucksack all week, but I was in such a state that I just couldn't bring myself to finish his story. And Granddad had hardly mentioned it. By the look of him, I'd say he'd been just as preoccupied as I was.

'Sorry, Granddad. I've had . . . stuff on my mind.'

'Yes I can see that,' he said, 'but you *have* to finish it. I can't rest until I've put the record straight. I want you to know the truth.'

'Couldn't you just tell me now?'

'I don't think so.'

'Come on, Granddad. I'd really like to hear the rest of the story.'

'Well, I suppose . . .' When he was quite satisfied that no one was hiding behind the portable lavatory thing, he turned to me and nodded. 'Where had you got to, m'boy?'

'You were just about to join your ship.'

'Ah yes,' he said, struggling to haul himself up the north face of his pillows. 'We boarded *HMS Thanatos* in Algiers. I remember thinking how thin the armour looked. Almost like a sardine tin. Of course cruisers are built for speed and don't carry extra weight like thick-skinned battleships.'

'Yes, but what happened, Granddad?'

'As Captain Brady said, we'd hardly had time to sling our hammocks before we were racing up to Taranto to bombard the Italian coast. Those five-and-half inch guns made a hell of a racket. Rather like a high explosive going off in a dustbin.'

'What about the —?'

'Did I mention the food?'

'No, Granddad.'

'Actually it wasn't at all bad, considering.' A distant light gleamed in his bloodshot eyes. 'Herrings in tomato sauce, Soya Links, ship's biscuits, of course – I was rather fond of them. And if you were really desperate you could always get hold of some nutty from the NAAFI.'

'What's nutty?'

'Naval chocolate; rather like eating solidified cocoa, though, strangely, completely lacking in nuts.'

'Tell me about Tommy Riley, Granddad. How did he take to being at sea?'

'Like a duck to water, oddly enough. We all had our action stations, of course. Tommy was clever, potential officer material. So they gave him a job down below in the transmitting station.'

'How about you, Granddad?'

'I was a look-out on the bridge, and Sharky Beal was my reader.'

'Reader?'

'Yes. I sat behind a pair of binoculars fixed to a scale. Whenever I spotted an enemy plane I had to yell "aircraft". Sharky's job was to read off the angles so that our guns could fix on the target. He wasn't too happy about that.'

'Why not?'

'He didn't think he'd see much action "hiding behind a bleedin' pair of binoculars". Mind you, they were a magnificent piece of engineering.'

'How do you mean?'

'They were so powerful that when you looked into the

distance you could actually see that the world was round. If you sighted a ship on the horizon, its stern was bent over the curvature, almost as if it was sliding off the edge of the world.'

He yawned and slid a little further down his pillows.

'Yes, but what's the big secret, Granddad? I thought you wanted to tell me about it.'

The war wound under his left eye was gently weeping. It still did that sometimes, even after more than fifty years.

'It all started when we went down to Alexandria for a boiler clean. That's where we had the photograph taken. The funny thing is, I can hardly bear to look at it now.'

'Why's that?'

'I suppose because it reminds me of the last time in my life when I was truly happy.'

'What happened, Granddad? Please, you've got to tell me.'

He stared into the distance. 'It was the first time we saw some real action. You see, the three of us were playing cards when . . . when . . .'

'Granddad, Granddad . . . Granddad?'

His head fell onto his chest and he let out a ghostly howl.

'Wake up, Granddad. At least tell me the end of the . . .'

It was something he used to do when I was little: pretend to fall asleep in the middle of the story just to check I was listening. Then he'd spring back to life and make me jump. But this time it was for real. I knew I shouldn't wake him, so I cradled his head in my hands and lifted it gently onto the pillow.

Just as I was tiptoeing to the door, I got this silly urge to do something I hadn't done for ages. Granddad preferred a firm handshake or a pat on the back, but there wasn't a lot he could do about it. I leaned across and kissed his sandpapery cheek. He smelled of that funny soap they used to have at Nanny's house.

'Goodbye, Granddad. See you tomorrow.'

6.18 p.m.
Mum had promised she'd be out by half five at the latest, but the engaged sign was still up on her office door and every now and then the sound of raised voices spilled out into the empty corridor.

Dad's mobile was off again, so I left him yet another message: 'Hi Dad, me again. Sorry, but I'm really worried about Granddad. He looked so ill today. And he keeps telling me he's going to . . . Can *you* talk to him? Please, Dad . . . Oh and Dad – good luck for the race tomorrow.'

I tried to keep my mind off the *Belfast* trip by playing Tetris on my phone. But all I could think about was what a perfect place a World War Two cruiser was for someone to meet with a 'nasty accident'. My imagination turned somersaults until I'd been through every single worse case scenario in the *Seaman's Handbook*.

And that's when it struck me that I'd need all the friends I could get the next day. Only Abby and Dimbo were really talking to me. I was a total Billy no mates. I knew it was a long shot, but seeing as he hadn't replied to any of my texts,

I thought it might just be worth a try. I tapped in his home number, squeezed hard on my blob of Blu-Tack and pressed dial.

'Yeah, waddayouwant?' said a half-familiar voice.

'Is that Mrs Pitts?'

She sounded weird. 'Who is it wants to know?'

'It's Sam, Sam Tennant.'

The Wicked Witch of the West transformed into Mary Poppins. 'Oh Sammy, how lovely to hear from you.'

'Is Alex there?'

'No,' she said, turning back into a witch again. 'Alex and Molly are with their father.'

'Do you know when he'll be back?'

'How long does it take to choose an engagement ring?'

'What?'

'He wanted the children to feel part of it. Sick, isn't it?'

'Well, I —'

'Apparently they're going to conduct the whole disgusting charade on a beach in Mauritius. Do you know where *we* got married, Sammy?'

'In a church?'

'Hackney Registry Office.' She laughed, but it didn't sound like she found it all that funny.

'Do you think you could ask Alex to call me when he gets in, please?'

'Well, I'll do my best, but if he's half as slippery as his father you might as well hire a private detective. Did I tell you about —?'

'OKthanksbye.'

Mr and Mrs Pitts used to take us bowling. Sometimes they got really cross with each other about the scoring. I knew Alex liked all the presents and stuff, but I had a feeling he was still sort of hoping they might get back together again. Maybe he was only avoiding me because he didn't want to talk about the wedding.

Mum's meeting was going on forever. The kid in there must have been a right psycho. Even the pyromaniac boy wasn't that full on. I was so hungry that I took out the remains of Granddad's sherbet fountain. But after a couple of sucks I felt really guilty. His story seemed to be whispering at me from the bottom of my rucksack. I knew I'd promised him I'd finish it. The trouble was, part of me really needed to find out what happened, and another part was terrified of reading something I didn't want to hear.

What was so good about the truth anyway? Wasn't it better to believe what you wanted to believe? My hand hovered above my rucksack while I tried to decide.

Sliding Off
the Edge of the World

The three of us were having a quiet game of cards, when the peace was shattered by the dreaded sound of the action station rattlers and the crackle of the tannoy: 'D'you hear there, d'you hear there? Close up to action stations. Close up to action stations.'

'Gonna see some action,' said Sharky grimly. 'Gonna make my family proud.'

I struggled into my anti-flash gear (white asbestos gloves and hoodie, designed to protect from burns) in record time. Tommy on the other hand seemed more concerned with his lifejacket.

I can still hear the ring of boots on iron ladders, the full-throated cursing and whispered prayers, as all hands hurried to action stations. It's funny what goes through your head at a time like that, but I remember thinking what a tragedy it would be if I copped it having never tasted lobster.

It was a clear blue Mediterranean afternoon when Sharky and I arrived on the bridge. You could almost have imagined we were on a pleasure cruise; only the ping of the asdic (anti-submarine device) and the distant drone of a squadron of Junkers 88s gave the game away.

Suddenly, there they were in the corner of the sky, six of them in formation, small grey dots in my binoculars, which rapidly became fully-fledged warplanes.

'Aircraft!' I shouted.

Sharky read off the angles and our guns swung round to face them like angry Daleks.

One by one, they peeled away from their formation and swooped. I can't tell you what that feels like, Sam, to have an enemy plane screeching towards you at two hundred miles per hour with four thousand pounds of high-explosives on board, but I can promise you one thing: I was absolutely terrified.

Captain Brady on the other hand, was a picture of serenity, waiting for precisely the right moment to return their fire.

Every gun on the Thanatos opened up. It was awesome in the true sense of the word, a deafening cacophony, which quadrupled in intensity when every other ship in the convoy opened up too.

But it wasn't enough. Undaunted by the big guns and a barrage of ack-ack fire, one of the planes was hurtling towards us at an impossible angle. I started praying as he moved in for the kill. But at the last minute, the pilot pulled out of his dive, peppering the deck with bullets and unleashing a brace of bombs, which whistled through the air and exploded in the sea with a muffled crackle.

Our sister ship, the Erebos, wasn't so lucky. Dense clouds of yellow smoke were pouring from her funnel.

And again they came. It was many years before I could appreciate the pilot's bravery, pulling out of his dive even later this time, risking death to deliver his bombs on target. Everyone on the bridge hit the floor as the roar of his twin engines rose above the thunder of our own five-and-a-quarter inch guns. And I realised that what I had taken for flying debris was actually the sound of machine-gun bullets ricocheting off the deck.

A brilliant white flash preceded the mother of all explosions, and I knew instantly we'd been hit. Of course I should have been focusing on the task in hand, but it was impossible to ignore the scenes of devastation. A-turret was a raging inferno. Rescue teams of stokers raced towards it, hoses at the ready, and the sick-berth tiffies began hauling out the screaming survivors.

There are some things no man should ever see. The starboard Oerlikon gunner, a Welsh lad by the name of Meredith, was slumped across the pedestal, brains oozing like raspberry ripple.

'He's coming back to finish us off,' said Sharky, staring blankly into the sky. 'What the bleedin' hell am I doing here?'

He was the last man I'd expected to desert his post. It was a court-martial offence, and besides, if anyone was going to 'funk it', it would probably be me. But as the bomber prepared for another run, Sharky was nowhere to be seen.

They say that when the tiger has you in his jaws, a sense of resignation sets in. Our biggest gun was out of action, the port pom-pom platform was shot to bits and ferocious flames were licking the quarterdeck. As our tormentor plummeted towards us again like a turbo-charged vulture, I knew in my heart that lobster was permanently off the menu.

I didn't recognise him at first, the small, determined figure who appeared on the quarterdeck, fighting his way through a procession of stretcher-bearers to get to the Oerlikon gun. It was only after he'd released Meredith from the waste-belt, eased himself onto the shoulder supports and grabbed hold of the trigger that I realised who he was.

No one will ever know for certain who bagged the JU88 and sent her, belching black smoke, into the clear blue sea, but I like to think it was Sharky. Though mortally wounded, he kept firing till the last, and had it not been for the 'irregular circumstances' they would surely have given him a medal.

By some miracle, the planes did not return. A cheer went up when Broadside Brady announced we were abandoning our mission and returning to Alexandria.

The next morning, I joined one of the hose parties, scraping gobbets of flesh from the deck with a shovel, trying to wash away the nauseating odour of dried blood that was baked into the twisted metal by the blistering sun. And to keep our spirits up we whistled the songs from Snow White.

'Who wants a tickler?' said a battle-hardened Leading Seaman, brandishing a bloodstained packet of cigarettes. 'They were Meredith's. He won't want them now.'

That afternoon, we buried our dead; all eighteen of them, stitched into their hammocks and shrouded in the union flag. The marines fired a volley, a bugler played 'The Last Post', and the ship's chaplain told us what an honour it was to die for our country. Tommy and I watched from the quarterdeck as our old friend Sharky slid slowly into the sea.

'I suppose he got what he was looking for in the end,' said Tommy. 'He was always saying he wanted to see some action.'

'We should write to his family,' I said, secretly hoping that Tommy would volunteer for the job. 'They'll be so proud when they hear how brave he was.'

Tommy shook his head. 'Sharky didn't have any family.'

'What do you mean?'

'Didn't he tell you? They all copped it in the Blitz. He came from fire-watching one night and his house was just a pile of rubble. All that was left was the aspidistra. He said he couldn't understand why God would let his three kid sisters be blown to smithereens, but save a stupid pot plant.'

It was twenty years before I tasted lobster, in a little bed and breakfast on the Dorset coast. I found it chewy and rather flavourless, and I couldn't help thinking of poor old Sharky. But at least he died a hero. At least he'd done something to be proud of. I only wish I could say the same thing.

And so to the hard part, the part I've been dreading since I started. Please believe me when I tell you that it was never my intention to keep it a secret. Many's the time I tried to share my shame with your grandmother, but whenever I came to the end of the story, I got so churned up inside that I couldn't find the words. I like to think she would have forgiven me. I hope, Samuel, you will find it in your heart to do likewise.

6.35 p.m.

Mum stuck her head round the door and almost managed a smile. 'How are you doing?'

To tell you the truth, I wasn't doing that great. I'd been kind of hoping that courage ran in my genes, but I was beginning to wonder if it was ever there in the first place.

'Are you going to be long, Mum?'

'We're just coming out now.'

'Good. I really want to get home.'

'The thing is,' said Mum, fiddling with the squidgy brain worry ball that she'd got from the drugs rep, 'would you mind popping into the communal waiting room? It's all right, there's no one in there.'

'What for?'

'Just do it, Sam, there's a good lad.'

'But why?'

She closed the door behind her and put on her 'professional counsellor' voice. 'All right, look, the child I've been seeing goes to your school.'

'Who is it?'

'You know I can't tell you that. And I'm sure the last thing they'd want is for you to know who they are.'

'I'll close my eyes, OK?'

'Come on, love. If you don't make a fuss, we'll pick up a Chinese on the way home.'

'OK then.'

The communal waiting room stank of disposable nappies, damp old people and screwed-up teenagers. I gazed down on the deserted car park (all that was left were Mum's little hatchback and a grey beast of a people-carrier), trying not to think about the next day, trying to convince myself that everything was going to be all right.

Granddad's story was screaming at me, like a ventriloquist's dummy: '*Let me out, let me out!*' But I had a nasty feeling I wouldn't get the happy ending I'd been hoping for. I still wanted to believe in Granddad the war hero.

The noticeboard above the smelly sandpit was a random reminder that other people had problems too. It was covered with helplines for addictions I've never even heard of and cartoons of lonely pensioners and children in wheelchairs. It ought to have made me feel better, but it didn't.

And then it hit me. What had started as a whisper in the back of my head suddenly turned into a full-throated roar: WHAT ARE YOU, STUPID OR SOMETHING?

It was so obvious. Why hadn't I thought of it before? Mum words were taking on a whole new meaning: '*I'm sure the last thing they'd want is for you to know who they are.*' Of course they wouldn't. Especially if they were The . . .

It all made perfect sense. That kid, the one Mum was having so much trouble with, the one she'd been scared might do 'something stupid'. It just had to be – there was no other possible explanation. Mum's client from hell was The Emperor.

I charged to the window, crunching through a minefield of Lego and plastic fruit in a desperate attempt to get a glimpse of him. But it was too late. All I could see was the grey people-carrier pulling out of the car park.

6.50 p.m.

'Look, for the last time,' said Mum, trying to find her favourite DJ on the car radio, 'I can't tell you, Samuel, so just leave it, OK?'

'Come on, Mum, it's important.'

'What, so you can spread it round the school, you mean?'

'No, it's not —'

'God, I love Sting. They played this at our wedding disco.'

'Wedding what?'

She didn't know the words, but it didn't stop her singing along in an embarrassing, squeaky voice.

'Mum, please. Look, I wouldn't tell anyone, I promise.'

'Was that your phone, Sam? Might be your girlfriend.'

Must have been Alex returning my texts. At least something was going right.

'Come on then, Sammy, what's it to be: pizza or Chinese?'

'I'm sorry, I'm not hungry.'

Mum started going into a comedy routine about me not being hungry making it onto the Ten o'Clock News, but I didn't hear her because I was too busy staring into my mobile.

As usual, The Emperor's message was short and to the point.

U R SO DEAD

FRIDAY
(WEEK TWO)

9.15 a.m.

Mum had an emergency meeting with the social worker, so she dropped me fifteen minutes early.

'There's something I really need to tell you, Mum.'

'Sorry love, I've got a taxi up my bum. It'll have to wait.'

The booming gobbledegook from the station tannoy was making me shiver. 'I've got this terrible stomach ache.'

'You're just excited, Sammy. Trust me, you'll be fine when you get on the train.'

'No, Mum, I don't —'

The taxi driver started beeping.

'All right, all right, keep your hair on, baldy!' Mum reached across and opened my door. 'Hurry up, Sam. I want to leave your dad a good-luck message before his race.'

'You don't understand. I think they're —'

'Now don't forget, when you arrive back, you're going to walk straight to your granddad's. So I'll see you at the usual time, OK?'

As soon as Mum mentioned Granddad I started feeling guilty. I'd been so busy worrying about The Emperor that I still hadn't finished his story. But at least thinking about him had given me the courage I needed to get out of the car.

'Yes . . . fine . . . see you at the usual time.'

'I've put a Capri Sun and some Cheesy Wotsits into a brown-paper bag in the front of your rucksack,' said Mum, sticking an arm out of the window and jabbing her index finger at the sky. 'Don't throw the bag away, I can recycle it.'

We were supposed to meet underneath the TV screens in the ticket hall. Much to my relief, I couldn't see any of my tormentors, just some random Year Eights free-running up the side of the photo booth, a circle of girls auditioning new ringtones, a couple of unsuspecting parent helpers and Mr Peel hiding behind a magazine called *NME*.

Dimbo would have made a terrible spy. His briefcase was a dead giveaway. 'Psst! Over here, next to the newspapers.'

'Where is everybody?'

'You know our contemporaries, Samuel. Punctuality is hardly their strong point.'

'Did you find anything else online?'

'No. That Chickenboyz website has completely vanished.'

'What would they do that for?'

Dimbo shrugged and peeled his Kit Kat. 'Destroying the evidence perhaps? But it's probably nothing. Just stick to the plan and you'll be fine.'

'Are you sure about that?'

'I know the exact points on the platform where the train doors open. If you stand next to me, I'll make sure you get on first. It'll give you a head start.'

The unmistakable sound of Callum Corcoran's laughter was strutting up Station Road.

'What do I do now?'

'Go and talk to old Peel,' said Dimbo, gobbling down his final finger of Kit Kat. 'Get him started on the "music business". He'll bore you to death, but at least you'll be safe from The Emperor.'

'But I don't know anything about . . .'

They swept into the ticket hall, like the local hunt: Pete Hughes looking cool, Gaz Lulham trying to copy him, Chelsea sticking a square of Elastoplast over her nose stud, Callum and Animal kicking a dead Coke can, plus virtually half my tutor group in a state of high excitement, which rose to fever pitch the moment they spotted me.

'There he is,' shouted a voice from the back. 'Hope he's wearing swimming trunks.'

'Let's find out,' said Animal, advancing menacingly.

'Is that magazine any good, Sir?' I said, sidling up to Mr Peel before they could get any closer.

He was wearing that leather jacket he'd worn for

Parents' Evening. 'Just having a squint at this year's "cool list" – have you seen it yet?'

'Er . . . no, not yet.'

Old Peel looked quite relieved. He smiled wistfully as my 'classmates' paraded around the ticket hall flapping imaginary wings and making chicken noises. 'Look at them. The best years of their lives and they don't even know it. God, I wish I was a kid again! Not a care in the world. Isn't that right?'

A massive cheer went up when Mr Catchpole and Miss Stanley walked into the station side by side.

'You been car-sharing, Miss?' said Chelsea. 'That's good for the environment that is, Miss. Is he a good . . . *driver*, Miss?'

Mr Catchpole swatted angrily at a wasp with his timetable. 'Yes, thank you Chelsea, I'll do the funnies. And may I remind those of you who seem determined to turn the station into a farmyard,' that all the time you are in school uniform you are representatives of the school. Now, form an *orderly* queue, and in a moment, we'll proceed, quickly and *quietly*, onto the platform.'

During the ensuing chaos, I saw Alex slope into the ticket hall with another new rucksack over his shoulder. For a second, our eyes met, but he swiftly turned his attention to a vodka advert and my spirits sank a little further.

Things improved significantly when, a few seconds later, Abby appeared, stepping carefully through the carnage and quietly joining the end of the queue. Her hair looked good with that plastic thingy keeping it out of her face, and the smile that flickered across it when she saw me was just what the doctor ordered.

9.53 a.m.

'The train shortly arriving at platform seven is the First Capital Connect service for London Bridge, calling at . . .'

'Don't forget,' whispered Dimbo, 'I'll text you if the ticket collector's coming.'

I stared at the dot in the distance, trying to ignore the random chorus of insults from the other end of the platform, poised behind the yellow line like a sprinter waiting for the starting pistol. 'Dimbo?'

'What is it?'

'Thanks.'

As the train rumbled into the station, I ran through one of those 'creative visualisations' that Dad did before every race, picturing myself leaping into the carriage and darting along the central aisle. I was halfway to First Class when I felt a cold hand on the back of my neck.

'What the . . . ?'

Looking up, I realised that the front of the train was bearing down on me. Just for a nanosecond, I lost balance, teetering precariously on the wrong side of the yellow line.

'Oh, it's *you*. Thank goodness for that. I thought some-one was trying to . . .'

'I wanted to wish you luck, Sam,' she said, blushing slightly. 'I've been really worried about you.'

'Thanks, Abby.'

'I don't know what they're planning, but I heard one of them say something about waiting for The Emperor's signals. You will be careful, won't you, Sam?'

The train doors were directly in front of me, just like Dimbo said they would be. 'Got to go,' I said, preparing to jump. 'I'm going to sneak into First Class.'

She nodded thoughtfully.

'Hey, Abby?'

'Yes.'

'You haven't forgotten what I asked you about earlier?'

'No,' she said, her face pinkening. 'I hadn't forgotten.'

'Hurry up, you idiot,' hissed Dimbo. 'The doors are opening.'

'Is it a yes or a no, Abby?'

But I didn't have time to wait for her answer. Down at the other end of the platform, Mr Catchpole was trying to hold back the hordes.

'One at a time, please. And no pushing.'

I jumped onto the 9.43 for London Bridge and hit the ground running.

After about twenty minutes, I started to relax. The first-class compartment was completely empty, and the toilet was just down the corridor, so I knew there was somewhere to hide in an emergency. Best of all, nobody had come looking for me.

I slipped further into my comfy seat, not counting my chickens exactly, but confident enough to rest my eyes for a second.

Whether it was the motion of the train or the fact I'd hardly slept for a week, I'm not sure. All I know is that somewhere between Gatwick Airport and East Croydon, I must have dozed off.

BIG MISTAKE.

10.16 a.m.
What made it ten times more terrifying was their silence. Not one of them uttered a single word. From the moment I awoke to discover I was blind, until it was all over, the only sounds I could make out were the rattle of the train, a few stifled giggles and a crackly mobile playing R'n'B.

Half asleep still, and longing to return to my soothing slumbers, I became dimly aware of a thin band tightening around my head. Next came the blackness. I tried to open my eyes, but they were prisoners in their own sockets. 'Help me, please, I . . . I can't see.'

Somebody grabbed my hand as it flew up to my face to investigate. 'What's happening? Get off me I . . .'

And suddenly I was wide awake.

They dragged me from my seat and manhandled me down the aisle. 'Leave me alone,' I screamed. 'You mustn't —' A sticky hand that smelled of peppermints clamped itself across my mouth and I stopped trying to fight back. What was the point? There were just too many of them and the more I kicked out, the harder my invisible tormentors kicked back.

But where were they taking me? And what were they going to do?

All became clear, when they bundled me into the cubicle and bolted the door. I knew instantly where we were. The smell was so overpowering I could hardly breathe. And I had a pretty good idea what they were planning too. Dad had told me all about 'bog-washing', but according to him it was something that died out with grammar schools.

'Please,' I whimpered. 'You can do anything, but not that.'

Blind panic seized me by the throat as they pushed me forward and started forcing my head down. I narrowed my nostrils, held my mouth tight shut and prepared for the unthinkable.

I could hardly believe it when my face made contact with the clean, cool water. It was the first bit of luck I'd had all week. Tommy Riley would have been terrified, but dunking my head in a sink full of water was something I'd been practising since primary school.

Instinctively I started counting; instantly my head began to clear.

Thirty-seven, thirty-eight, thirty-nine, forty . . .

But when were they going to stop? I was good, but I wasn't that good.

Fifty-seven, fifty-eight, fifty-nine, sixty . . .

My record was sixty-eight seconds. If I didn't breathe soon I could forget all about Year Nine.

Sixty-six, sixty-seven, sixty-eight, sixty-nine . . .

It came to me in a flash. Supposing they thought I was really hurt? Twitching dramatically, I gave up struggling and let my whole body go limp. And I could sense their panic as I slithered to the floor.

A second later, the door opened. I waited until the last one had fled, flinging my rucksack at me, and gulped in a massive mouthful of air. I was bruised and battered and soaking wet, but at least I was still breathing.

'What the hell do you think you're playing at?'

I'd never been so pleased to hear his voice. The blackness lifted. Looking up, I saw that Mr Catchpole was standing over me with a soggy school tie in his hand. 'And why's your hair so wet? Is there something you want tell me, Samuel?'

I automatically shook my head. It was totally dumb of me, but I hated the idea of old Catchpole knowing what a victim I was.

'Very well then,' he said, handing me a green paper towel. 'You'd better clean yourself up and follow me. I'm not letting you out of my sight for the rest of the journey.'

He frogmarched me down the aisle, through a mass of iPods and mobiles, of PSPs, Nintendo DSs and even a couple of antique Gameboys. None of my tormentors looked particularly guilty. Some of them even whispered 'words of encouragement' as I struggled to keep up with Mr Catchpole.

'Who's been a naughty boy then?' said Callum Corcoran.

'At least he doesn't smell of chicken poo no more,' said Chelsea.

Animal was almost crying with laughter. 'Listen to this,' he said, reading from the touch-screen of his mobile. 'You can't kill a chicken until you've given her a good wash.'

Pete Hughes was carefully re-gelling his hair. 'Wonder what The Emperor's got planned for the grand finale?'

But the most chilling comment of all came from a voice I didn't even recognise. 'You can run, Sam, but you can't hide.'

By the time we'd reached the teachers' ghetto, *I* was almost crying with despair.

Despair morphed into misery when I realised that the Dad Phone was blaring *Mission: Impossible*. That was the last thing I needed.

'Now sit down and be quiet,' said Mr Catchpole. 'Keep an eye on him, would you, Bryony? I think I saw some illegal substances back there.'

Miss Stanley was too engrossed in *Adventures for KS3 Geographers* to take any notice, but old Peel gave me a sympathetic nod before returning to his 'cool list'. I sneaked out my mobile, cradling it like a baby, trembling with trepidation, as I prepared to read my latest message. *What's up? Having a bad hair day?*

This time I was almost crying with relief. It was from Dimbo. (I should have realised from the punctuation.) There he was at the far end of the carriage, gnawing on a Pepperami and busily scribbling into his notebook. He looked up for a moment and nodded encouragingly. Who would have guessed that Dimbo would turn out to be my last hope?

Catchpole reappeared, brandishing a confiscated packet of cigarettes and two cans of Red Bull. 'Right, you'd better find something to read, boy. Have you got anything?'

'Only this Sir,' I said, unzipping my rucksack.

'What on earth's that?'

I'd promised myself I'd finish it by the next time I saw him. 'It's my granddad's war story, Sir.'

'Eye-witness accounts are a historian's goldmine,' said Mr Catchpole wistfully. 'Just make sure I don't hear a peep out of you for the rest of the journey.'

I'd been making all sorts of excuses not to read it. Perhaps fate was nudging me in the right direction.

Sliding Off
the Edge of the World

No one knew what was happening at first. The Thanatos listed violently to starboard and the mess-deck lockers swung open, unleashing a barrage of letters, photographs and more bizarrely, I seem to remember, a selection of Egyptian fezzes. Only when the water started rising in the lee scuppers did it become obvious we'd been 'tin-fished'.

Blind panic seized the mess deck. Old salts stuffed their pockets full of cigarettes, and a lad from Green Watch screamed hysterically for his mother. Some tried to rescue little treasures from home - a letter from the missus, a photograph of the kids, but everyone was gripped with the same passion, the passion to survive.

Everyone except Tommy that is; I couldn't believe his apparent coolness. He sat at the mess table, sucking an acid drop, the water lapping his ankles.

'Come on, Tommy,' I shouted. 'Get a move on.'

'I'm not coming, Ray.'

I was acutely aware of the stampede for the mess-deck ladder. 'There's nothing to be frightened of, you know. Come on, Tommy, get that bloody lifejacket on.'

He didn't move. 'I'm not frightened.'

'Then for God's sake pull yourself together,' I screamed. 'We've got to get out of here.'

'What's the point?' he said. 'You know I can't swim. Save yourself, Ray. It's the only logical thing to do.'

The water was already up to my knees. 'Look, I'll stay with you the whole time. We can do it together. I know we can.'

Poor Tommy; beneath the show of bravado, I suddenly saw that he was paralysed with fear. 'Promise you won't leave me, Ray?

'Swear on my mother's life.'

He nodded and reached for his lifejacket.

It was a starless night. The hiss of steam mingled with the tortured cries of the wounded, and a young subby (sub-lieutenant) was cutting away the Carley floats whilst another dashed about with a megaphone hollering 'Abandon ship!'

'Women and children first,' quipped a would-be comedian, as we started our ascent of the quarterdeck.

The further the Thanatos lurched to starboard, the more hazardous our climb became. Cascades of empty shell cases clattered towards us like a gigantic pinball machine.

At the top, we somehow managed to negotiate the port guardrail and ease ourselves onto the side of the ship. Scores of our shipmates were lining up to throw themselves into the sea.

'Come on in,' shouted the comedian, 'the water's lovely.'

We slid down as far the bilges, the barnacles gouging great grooves in my posterior. Darkness beckoned as we crouched side by side and prepared to leap into the unknown.

'I can't do it,' whispered Tommy.

'Of course you can. Now come on, I'll be with you all the way.'

I took his hand. He crushed my fingers in his vice-like grip. 'All right, Tommy, after three. One, two . . .'

But the Thanatos was in her death throes. A colossal explosion blasted us into the air and the next thing I knew I was being dragged underwater by the sinking ship. Twice she pulled me down; twice I managed to claw my way to the surface and spew out a mouthful of oily water.

'Tommy! Tommy! Where are you?' I bellowed.

Under different circumstances, it might have been a rather charming spectacle: hundreds of men, torches twinkling, bobbing about in the water. Some of them were scrambling aboard the Carley rafts and some were warbling that God-awful ditty 'Roll Out the Barrel'. I thrashed about in the inky-black water, hallooing Tommy's name and praying for a miracle.

The first corpse I encountered made me retch. By the time I came across the third I was quite adept at flipping them onto their backs and shining a light into their blue, lifeless faces. Pitiful as it was, I couldn't help heaving a sigh of relief every time I realised it wasn't Tommy. Something told me he was still alive; something told me I had a cat in hell's chance of finding him.

'Come on, Tommy, I know you're out there.'

The twinkling lights from the Carley rafts were slowly receding into the gloom. I needed to find him, and find him fast.

'Come on, Tommy, give us a shout.'

It seemed like a miracle. His voice was breathy and weak, but I would have recognised it anywhere. 'Ray . . . Ray . . . Is that you, Ray?'

'Don't worry, Tommy. I'm coming to get you.'

And there he was, clinging to a piece of driftwood. He winced as my torch beam caught him full in the face. 'You took your time.'

I wanted to give him a big hug. But as you know, I've never been a great one for unnecessary displays of affection.

'Come on, you ungrateful bugger, let's get the hell out of here.'

His voice grew feebler by the second. 'Promise you'll stay with me, Ray.'

'Of course I will, but we need to get a move on. Those lifeboats aren't going to hang around forever, you know.'

How swiftly elation can turn to despair. All thoughts of an improbable happy ending vanished instantly when my torch picked out the gaping hole in his chest that was spouting blood. I didn't need a doctor to tell me he was dying. No man on earth could have survived such a wound.

And yet somehow he managed to smile. 'What are you crying for? Not going soft on me are you, Ray?'

'I'm not crying,' I said, my salt tears mingling with the oil and seawater. 'I'm laughing.'

They were tears of frustration. 'Roll Out the Barrel' was fading into the distance. Fate had presented me with the starkest of choices: either keep my promise and stay with Tommy until the bitter end, or make a break for the lifeboats and save myself before it was too late.

The next time I saw Tommy was in the 68th General Hospital in Alexandria. I couldn't understand why he was already up and about while I was still languishing in bed. After all, I was one of the lucky ones; most of the poor devils on the ward were burns victims, smothered from head to toe in gentian violet and reeking of blistered pork, whereas all I had was mild exposure and a sore bum.

It was such a relief to see him. But I couldn't understand why his face was still covered in oil. And I couldn't understand why no one had thought to dress his wound, which was still spouting blood. Nor could I comprehend his stony silence - how he stood at the bottom of the bed and simply beckoned.

And suddenly he was gone.

I screamed for the nurse. Why had my old oppo walked out on me without even saying goodbye? She smiled professionally and said I must be mistaken. It was the middle of the night. Visiting hours were between two p.m. and three-thirty. Besides, if he really was such a 'good chum', he was sure to be back tomorrow.

The nurse was right - Tommy visited me

every night for a week, standing at the bottom of my bed and beckoning reproachfully, until one afternoon, a gunner from the Thanatos confirmed what I already knew: that 'the Professor' was dead.

On my next leave, I went to see Tommy's parents. I told them how brave he'd been, how lucky I was to have had such a good friend and how life would never be the same without him. But I didn't tell them how he'd died, how I was the coward who'd condemned him to a cold and lonely death, and how I'd never forget the look he gave me when he realised I was deserting him.

As we parted, I presented his mother with a copy of the photograph we'd had taken in Alexandria, and she gave me a quarter of sherbet lemons for the return journey. Stumbling into the blackout, I tripped and fell, cutting my face on a broken milk bottle. I didn't actually tell anyone it was a war wound, they simply assumed it. And my dear old mum was so proud of me that I never had the heart to tell her I'd got it running for the twenty-seven bus. Some war hero, eh, Sam?

To begin with, I thought about Tommy every

day. Fortunately for my sanity, it didn't last. But before every important moment in my life (first job, wedding day, children, retirement - grandchildren, of course) I'd have these vivid dreams about him. And just occasionally, I fancied I'd spotted his face in a crowd, though of course whilst I got older, Tommy was forever eighteen.

So I knew exactly what was going to happen when I started dreaming about him again. Just as I also knew that if I didn't tell someone what really happened that night our ship went down, I'd never be able to die in peace.

10.40 a.m.

'For goodness' sake boy, put that thing away.'

I stared at the last paragraph, wishing literally *and* metaphorically that it wasn't the end of the line.

'Interesting, was it?' said Mr Catchpole.

Now that I'd finished Granddad's story, I had a nasty feeling that the only thing running in my genes was running itself. All I could manage was a dazed, 'Yes, Sir.'

'You hear that, Bryony?' said Mr Catchpole, fumbling in the luggage rack for his Tesco bag. 'A St Thomas's child who actually professes an interest in reading.'

'Yeah, nice one,' said old Peel, winking at Miss Stanley and squidging his coffee cup. 'I thought *you* were the one who did the funnies, Colin.'

Most of 8SE were already on the platform, pressing their faces against our carriage window, like a gallery of ghouls. And one of them, if only I'd known who it was, had scrawled YOU R SO DEAD! in the dust.

'Come on, Samuel, you're keeping everyone waiting,' said Miss Stanley. 'Why don't you go and join your friends?'

'Oh, I don't think so,' said Mr Catchpole. 'We don't want him wandering off again, do we? You'd better walk with Miss Stanley and me – and no more funny business.'

I didn't care about the squawking and barrage of random abuse that greeted me when I stepped onto the platform flanked by my two sour-faced minders, because for the next ten minutes at least, I was safe.

'Now, do *not* make me shout,' shouted Mr Catchpole.

'And for goodness' sake, keep still while Miss Stanley does a head count.'

'Better look out for Sam Tennant, Miss,' said Pete Hughes, putting an imaginary revolver to his head and pulling the trigger. 'I think he might be about to lose his.'

Mr Catchpole led our ragged crocodile along the riverside walkway, past swathes of sweaty joggers, cool London kids on skateboards who even made Pete Hughes look dorkish, aluminium-tabled sushi restaurants and an old man and his dog lying behind a felt-tipped message on a scrap of cardboard: *PLEASE HELP ME. I'M DESPERATE.*

I knew exactly what he meant. Looking across at the bleak outline of the Tower of London, I was starting to feel like the condemned man. But at least Anne Boleyn *knew* she was going to get her head chopped off. I hadn't a clue what was waiting for me.

'Why are they so quiet?' I whispered. 'What are they going to do next?'

Dimbo was two paces behind me, peeling an orange. 'No one seems to know. They're waiting for another signal from The Emperor.'

'What?'

'Don't worry, I've got a hunch who it might be.'

'You said you hadn't the faintest idea.'

'I'm sure you remember Sherlock Holmes's theory,' he said rather smugly. 'When you have eliminated the impossible, whatever remains, *however improbable*, must be the truth.'

'All right, who is it then?'

'I need to check something first, but I'll let you know as soon as I'm absolutely certain.'

'Well, get on with it. They could have killed me back there.'

A sarcastic 'oooohhh' went up when we came to a halt in front of the *Belfast*. But even though she was pretty impressive (six enormous guns pointing to the sky) I didn't give her a second glance, just stared into the murky green water, hardly able to believe that only two weeks ago I'd actually been looking forward to this.

12.30 p.m.

I was far too scared to eat, but after the others had finished their packed lunches and we'd sat through what would normally have been a fairly interesting presentation on the D-Day Landings, Mr Catchpole led us up to the quarterdeck for a 'final briefing'.

'Right,' he said. 'Can anyone tell me what we're actually here for?'

'To strangle a chicken?' suggested a voice from the back.

'We are here to consider the reality of war,' said Mr Catchpole. 'And while we are doing so, may I remind you once again that the good name of St Thomas's Community College is at stake. Do I make myself clear?'

Callum Corcoran clicked his heels together and gave a Nazi salute. *'Ya mein Führer!'*

'Right, Corcoran, that's a detention,' said Mr Catchpole, glancing for approval at the man in naval uniform who checked the tickets. 'Now, we will meet back here at one-thirty precisely. And woe betide the foolish individual who keeps me waiting.

'But before you go, I think we should have two minutes' silence, two minutes' silence in which to consider what it might have been like to serve on the *Belfast* in time of war. Imagine if you will, a young man, not much older than yourselves, away from home for the first time, and faced with the very real prospect of never returning.' He checked his watch. 'Two minutes' silence, starting from . . . *now*.'

In just one hundred and twenty seconds, it would be every man for himself. I took one last peep at the prime suspects: Callum and Animal having a spitting competition into the Thames, Gaz Lulham and Chelsea checking their mobiles and giggling furtively, Pete Hughes fixing me with a sinister smile, and someone at the back whistling the Death March. I didn't want to admit it, but I was no closer to identifying The Emperor than when this whole nightmare began.

And then I saw that Dimbo was frantically trying to attract my attention. He was trapped behind a posse of girls, standing on tiptoes, waving his notebook at me. If only I'd been a lipreader, because he was mouthing a word that I just couldn't make out. It looked like 'happy', but what could that mean? I certainly didn't feel happy, and come to think of it, Dimbo didn't have that much to be delirious about either.

'Right,' said Mr Catchpole. 'I hope that was instructive. Now, in a moment I'm going to ask you to lead off in an *orderly* fashion. Just follow the arrows, it's very well signposted.'

Dimbo tried to push his way through the crowd towards me, using his briefcase as a battering ram.

'Did I tell anyone to move?' roared Mr Catchpole. 'No, Sir, I did not. And you ought to know better, Stephen Allbright. Stay right where you are and don't move a muscle until I say so.'

'Dimbo's forgotten his calculator,' shouted an anonymous comedian.

Mr Catchpole hoisted his Tesco bag aloft in a vain attempt to quell the general hilarity. 'Mr Peel and the parent helpers are already patrolling the decks. But as you can see, The *Belfast* is such a huge vessel that they can't possibly be everywhere at once. So, rather than trying to police the whole lot of you, Miss Stanley and I will set up camp in the Walrus Café, where we will be available should you have any *reasonable* queries.'

Was it possible to get seasick on a stationary ship? I'd been counting on sticking like glue to 'I'll do the funnies', but if he was having tea for two with Miss Stanley I might just as well hand myself over to The Emperor and have done with it. My only hope was to find a good hiding place and lie low until one-thirty. If only I could remember more about that virtual tour.

'Off you go then,' said Mr Catchpole. 'And don't forget, imagine what it would be like to be completely terrified.'

12.36 p.m.
I raced down the gloomy corridor, past the shipwright's

office and the chapel, across the red-and-white checked lino. It reeked of floor polish, and wherever you turned there was a pasty-faced waxwork of a World War Two sailor and the disembodied voices of Churchill and Vera Lynn on continuous loop.

But that wasn't Churchill, and it certainly wasn't Vera Lynn. The unmistakable sound of the Corcoran laugh was stalking me. And like one of those dreams where your feet feel like concrete, it took all my strength to drag myself into the galley and duck down behind an angry-looking dummy, his meat cleaver hovering above a papier-mâché joint of beef.

'Where is he?' said Animal, coming far too close for comfort.

Callum Corcoran's non-regulation trainers appeared in the doorway. 'Probably wetting himself.'

It was too close to the truth to be half as funny as Animal seemed to think it was. 'Yeah, nice one, but what are we going to do with Chickenboy when we find him?'

Pete Hughes's classic Vans checkerboard slip-ons sauntered up to the silver Nike Elites. 'Make sure you've got your phones on. Wait for The Emperor's signal.'

'Why can't we just blap him?' said Animal.

'Because The Emperor's way will be well funny,' said Gaz Lulham. 'That website was legend.'

'Come on then,' said Callum Corcoran. 'Let's try outside. He can't have got far.'

I was letting out a sigh of relief that probably registered about 9.9 on the Richter scale when disaster struck.

It was my phone. The first few notes of the *Mission: Impossible* theme blasted out before my thumb reached the red button. What was Dimbo playing at?

'Did you hear that?' said Gaz Lulham.

'Hear what?' said Pete Hughes.

'I thought I heard music, didn't you?'

'It's Vera Lynn, you hufter,' said Pete Hughes.

'Vera who?' said Animal.

Pete Hughes sounded suspiciously like their commanding officer. 'Never mind that, let's get out of here.'

Which is exactly what I had to do; there was no way I could stay in that position for the next two hours. I needed somewhere else to hide. And from what I could remember of the virtual tour, I thought I knew the perfect place.

12.42 p.m.

Someone growled as I pushed past a party of foreign students. I mumbled *excusez-moi*, but there was no time for pleasantries if I wanted to find that safe haven.

And there it was – the huge airlock leading down to the engine room, which could pave the way for my miraculous escape. Only one thing was stopping me: the determined figure at the top of the ladder barring my way.

'Dimbo, what are you doing?'

'You can't go down there.'

'Why not? I've thought of a great place to hide.'

'No, you mustn't.'

'Please, you're in my way.'

I tried to push past him, but he stood firm, arms splayed like a crucifix. 'I'm sorry, Sam. I can't let you go down there.'

We glared at each other for what seemed like an ice-age, until a thought that had been bubbling away in the dark recesses of my mind exploded into the forefront of my consciousness. 'Oh my God.'

He grabbed hold of his briefcase. 'What's the matter?'

'It's you, isn't it?'

'Eh?'

And suddenly it was so obvious. Why hadn't I thought it of it before? 'You're The Emperor, aren't you?'

His chocolate-stained mouth formed what I realised was a self-satisfied smile. 'How did you work that one out?'

'What's that thing you said? When you've ruled out all the unlikely ones, the only answer is . . . How does it go? I mean, who else could have made that website? And why did you phone me just now when you knew they were looking for me?'

'Quite the little Sherlock Holmes, aren't we?'

'My mum's treated loads of kids like you.'

'I very much doubt it.'

'Just get out of my way.'

It felt good, the moment my fist made contact with his flabby stomach. Dimbo doubled up in pain. I pushed past him onto the first rung of the ladder.

'Sam,' he groaned. 'I need to tell you something.'

I'd heard enough from that freak to last me a lifetime. I slithered down the handrail, bumping to a halt on a narrow, green walkway. The bewildering network of giant, pipes and wheels and gauges stopped me dead in my tracks. I stood paralysed as the posh tones of the information monitor boomed up from below: '*HMS Belfast's propulsive machinery is laid out according to a system first introduced by the United States Navy . . .*'

A voice from above brought me back to my senses. 'Sam, come back. We need to talk.'

'Go away. Leave me alone.'

But it was no good. A second later, Dimbo stepped onto the ladder and started descending.

12.43 p.m.

There was only one way to go, and that was down. Where were those parent helpers when you really needed one? I clattered along the green walkway, the only thought in my head being to get as far away from that psycho as possible.

'Sam, wait,' he called. 'You don't understand.'

I understood all right. My lungs were in a terrible state, but I forced myself onwards because, after all the horrible stuff he'd done, Dimbo was probably capable of anything.

I threw myself down another iron ladder, my sweaty hands struggling to get a grip on the handrail. And that was it. I couldn't go any lower. Stumbling further into the gloomy labyrinth, past a notice reading, *You are now below the waterline*, I searched vainly for somewhere to hide and prayed for a miracle.

The moment I'd turned the corner, I realised the game

160

was up. Standing beneath the information monitor were two shadowy figures. Even from behind, I would have recognised those school blazers anywhere. Caught, like a rat in a trap, I cursed myself for letting Dimbo trick me into it.

His two accomplices turned slowly to face me and . . . and . . .

And maybe I believed in miracles after all. Relief flooded over me like a tidal wave and I was so happy I let out a sort of delighted chuckle. 'It's *you*!'

'Hello, Sam.'

It was funny to see them standing side by side. I didn't think they really knew each other. 'You have no idea how good it is to see you guys.'

'You too, Sam. We've been wondering where you'd got to.'

Dimbo was closing fast, but I didn't care any more; I felt sure that the three of us could see him off. 'I've been looking for somewhere to hide. Only it's not as easy as I thought.'

'Yes, I know,' Abby said, reaching into her shoulder bag. 'You can run, Sam, but you can't hide.'

'Tell me about it.'

And we all laughed, like the end of a cheesy sit-com.

'Oh by the way, Sam,' she said, handing me a small piece of white plastic. 'Present for you.'

It was like being reunited with an old friend. 'Wow, thanks, Abby, I didn't think I'd ever see it again.' And from the grin on Alex's face, I was guessing that my iPod nano wasn't the only friend I was going to be reunited with. 'But where did you find it?'

'In your rucksack,' said Abby.

'What?'

She rolled her eyes. 'You didn't even notice, did you?'

'Did it fall out or something?'

Dimbo staggered around the corner and collapsed in a heap, like Dad after his first quadrathon.

'You were too busy sobbing your little heart out about our website,' said Abby. 'It was like taking candy from a baby.'

I was so confused that when I opened my mouth it took a few seconds for the words to come out. 'You . . . *stole* . . . it? But what did you do that for?'

'Isn't it obvious?' said Abby. 'It's because we hate you, don't we, Lex?'

Alex nodded; my whole universe did a one-eighty degree flip.

As soon as I'd got my balance back, I started piecing together the details of this strange new world. 'It's you, it's you, isn't it, Abby? I can't believe it, *you're* The Emperor.'

'That's right. And my little step-brother-in-waiting here is Ollyg78.'

'That's what I've been trying to tell you,' groaned Dimbo. 'The first clue was her website. I thought I was the only one who was fluent in HTML. But then I remembered that online portfolio she made in IT.'

'Get on with it,' said Abby. 'We've got chicken to fry.'

'I couldn't understand why the message on the mirror was written in nail varnish,' continued Dimbo, 'and then when Catchpole was giving his speech just now, I realised who was wearing exactly the same colour, and it all fell into place. Look at her hands, Sam, look at her hands.'

Abby applauded sarcastically. 'Well done, Dimbo. Give the class genius a medal.'

I was still struggling to make sense of it all. 'What was all that about your stepbrother-in-waiting?'

'Yes,' said Abby, wrapping a strand of hair around her ring finger. 'Our mum and dad are getting married, aren't they, Lex? So rather than puke my guts up watching those two playing Mummies and Daddies, I thought we'd do something a bit more productive.'

'Picking on *me*, you mean?'

'Picking on you?' says Abby. 'You make it sound so tawdry. Come on, Sam, it was so much more spectacular than that.'

'But why? I thought you liked me!'

'That was the hardest part of all,' said Abby, a red film spreading like wildfire across her face and neck, 'pretending to be interested in a loser like you.'

I'd always assumed that Abby spent half her life blushing because she was so shy; I suddenly realised she was just *very* angry.

'Look, can we talk about this?' I said.

She threw back her head and laughed. 'You sound just like your mother. That bitch said I was mental.'

'My mum would never say anything like that.'

'It's true,' said Dimbo, struggling to his knees. 'She might be a bit unconventional, but Dr Tennant's an excellent therapist.'

'Shut up, you moron,' said Abby, planting her patent

163

leather ballerina pump in Dimbo's stomach. 'She really did my head in with her stupid questions: "*What sort of week have you had? Why are you so angry with your parents? How does that make you feel?*" The silly cow never knew when to stop. And what better way to get my own back on Sigmeena Freud than scaring the crap out of her darling little Harry Potter?'

'You've ruined my whole life.'

'I thought you listened to the *Shipping Forecast*, Chickenboy. He should have known he was in for a rough ride, shouldn't he, Lexie?'

Alex stared at the deck.

'But you've turned so many people against me.'

'Yes.' She smiled. 'And it was *so* easy – a few puerile jokes, a couple of cheap shots about your taste in music, and *bingo*! That idiot Catchpole keeps blathering on about "peer pressure", but all it took was a gentle nudge in the right direction and they were eating out of my hands.'

'But why?' I whispered. 'Why would they do that?'

'Oh it's amazing how motivating a shared hatred can be! Corcoran and his côterie just want to sit on their fat lazy arses all day, but find them a new victim and there's not one of them that won't go the extra mile. But you'd know about that, wouldn't you, Sam? Remember the time you said I reminded you of a nun?'

'I was trying to make you laugh.'

'And think of all the fun you had with "Brace Face".'

Alex hadn't said a word, but his ears were burning. He stood with his hands in his pockets, studying the floor through his new designer frames.

164

'What about you, Lex?' I said. 'We've been friends forever. My mum's always really nice to you.'

'Yes,' he mumbled, 'you and your perfect family.'

'I thought you liked my family.'

Alex shrugged. 'You had to rub it in, didn't you? All that stuff about my mum and dad's divorce, like it was a big joke or something. "Oh look, Lex has got a new MP4 player – wish *my* parents would split up!"'

'I didn't say that.'

'And you always acted like you were so much cleverer than me. Remember that mixing desk my mum bought me? You said I'd got about as much chance of becoming a DJ as Callum Corcoran has of winning the Nobel Peace Prize. But I didn't hear you laughing in the music block the other day. That Chickenboyz mix of mine scared you witless.'

I felt as if someone had just taken my whole life and flushed it down the lavatory. 'And that's what this is all about?'

'No one likes a smart arse, do they, Lexie?' said Abby, taking out her mobile.

'Look, I'm really sorry,' I said, knowing that in less than a minute I'd be sobbing uncontrollably. 'I didn't mean to upset either of you. I promise it won't happen again.'

'And you think that's the end of it, do you?' said Abby, her right thumb going into overdrive. 'Just wait until you hear about the grand finale, Samuel. All I have to do is text everyone on The Emperor's contacts list and my little posse will come running. I bet they can't wait to hear what I've got planned for you.'

Dimbo was rubbing his stomach. 'I should think very carefully about this if I was you, Abigail. You could find yourself in serious trouble. What would your parents say?'

'Like they give a toss,' said Abby, dangling her mobile under my nose as if daring me to grab it. 'No, this is it, sucker. All I have to do is . . . *damn*!'

'What's the matter?' said Alex.

'I'm losing my signal down here. You hold him while I go up on deck.'

Abby made for the ladder, but she didn't get more than a couple of steps before a brown leather missile scudded across the engine room, sending her and her mobile flying.

'Run, Sam, run!' shouted Dimbo.

'Stop him!' shrieked Abby, kicking away Dimbo's briefcase in disgust.

Alex grabbed me by the throat. 'Where do you think you're going, Chickenboy?'

I was so shocked by his betrayal that I could hardly move. From the corner of my eye, I saw Abby picking up her phone. This time there was no escape.

'Aww, diddums,' she said. 'Did poor little Sammy think his bestest mate was going to save him?'

Alex sniggered, and the rage that had simmered inside me finally exploded.

'You were supposed to be my friend!' I screamed, somehow finding the strength to lift him from his feet and fling him towards the advancing Abby. 'Friends are supposed to look out for each other.'

Freedom beckoned. I leapt onto the ladder and started

scrambling for the surface. And I was feeling pretty pleased with myself until Abby's shrill voice cut into me like a knife in the back. 'Hurry up, you moron, he's getting away!'

12.55 p.m.
It might have been hardwired into my genes, but by the time I reached the forward mess deck I'd been running so long my lungs were begging for mercy. I tried losing myself in a class of primary school kids, but I stood out like a giant at a convention of jockeys, and their teacher gave me such a dirty look that there was nothing for it but to carry on running.

Like Dad was always saying, I should have focused on the finishing line, because the moment I glanced back to check if they were still chasing me, I caught my foot in a chain and went flying.

My head hit the deck with a sickening thud and I watched, mesmerised, as a trail of red dots began forming on the white paintwork. For a moment, I thought they were spelling out some sort of coded message. And then I realised I was bleeding. Not tomato sauce this time, but thick, red, sticky blood.

'No, no, no, no, NO!' I scoured the deck with my sleeve, knowing that if I didn't destroy the evidence, I might just as well draw them a map with *X marks the spot*.

The waxwork figures at the mess-deck tables looked every bit as demoralised as I was, as if they were expecting an attack at any moment. Some were huddled over a never-ending game of dominoes, others poised perpetually above their tea mugs, whilst a grim-faced able-seaman recited a letter home in a dreary monotone. Even the ship's cat looked fed-up.

I staggered to my feet, swaying like a drunken sailor, desperate for somewhere to hide. If I could just find the strength to climb into one of those hammocks I might be safe for a bit. But it wasn't to be.

Maybe this was what being drunk felt like. I mean, it was the kind of thing that only happens in horror movies. So why was I so convinced that the waxworks were coming to life? I watched, transfixed, as a parade of uniformed figures stepped out of the gloom and formed a line in front of me. And I was sober again in an instant when I recognised the row of school ties – all at half-mast.

'Well, well, well,' said Callum Corcoran, so close I could almost taste his Hubba Bubba. 'Look who it isn't.'

The mess deck was filled with sounds of the chicken coop.

Chelsea was filming it all on her mobile. 'What's the matter with him? He can't even stand up straight.'

'Looks like concussion to me,' said Pete Hughes.

'How many fists am I holding up?' said Callum Corcoran.

This time I knew it was all over. There was no point pretending. 'All right, so you've found me. Just do what you have you to do and get it over with.'

Gaz Lulham looked at Callum. 'What *are* we going to do?'

'We're going to blap him, aren't we?' said Animal. 'Can I go first?'

'No!' said Pete Hughes. 'We've got to wait for The Emperor's signal.'

'Well, go on then,' said Chelsea.

For once in his life, Pete Hughes looked confused. 'What are you talking about?'

'You're The Emperor, aren't you?' said Chelsea. 'Tell us what to do.'

'No I'm not,' said Pete Hughes. 'I thought it was Callum.'

'But I thought it was Gaz,' said Callum.

'And I thought it was Chelsea,' said Gaz.

Animal looked disappointed. 'Why didn't anyone think it was me?'

And that's when their phones started ringing – a weird cacophony of Arctic Monkeys, that song off the Cadbury's advert, Kanye West, the *Austin Powers* theme and a solitary crazy frog.

They were all reaching confusedly for their mobiles when Abby burst into the mess, followed by her shifty lieutenant.

'Oi, Brace Face,' said Animal, silencing the last crazy frog ringtone in the western world. 'What are you doing here?'

Abby slipped back into silent nun mode. The others were inwardly digesting the contents of her latest text message. Whatever she had planned for me, it certainly wasn't pretty.

'You heard the man,' said Chelsea. 'Why are you following us?'

I was bursting to put them in the picture. 'It's her, Abby, she's The Emperor.'

'Shut up, Chickenboy,' said Callum Corcoran. 'We're not stupid, you know.'

'She couldn't be the Emperor anyway,' said Pete Hughes, slicking back his fringe. 'She's far too busy practising her precious saxophone.'

Dimbo looked like a heart-attack victim struggling into Casualty. 'It's true,' he panted. 'She *is* The Emperor. I've studied facts, and I can assure you, the evidence is conclusive.'

People didn't always understand Dimbo, but it was a well-established fact that he was always right.

'Thought it might be her,' said Gaz Lulham, unconvincingly.

'Yeah,' added Chelsea. 'She's got them evil eyes.'

'What kind of a person are you anyway?' said Pete Hughes, glaring reproachfully at Abby like he was the innocent victim of some cruel online hoax. 'I mean some of it might have been quite funny in a screwed-up sort of way, but did you honestly think we'd go *that* far?'

'We're not animals, you know,' said Animal.

'Are you sure about that?' muttered Abby. 'You morons have done everything else I've told you for the last two weeks – isn't that right, Lexie?'

Alex Pitts slunk further into the shadows.

'She's taken you all for a bit of a ride, hasn't she?' said Dimbo.

Callum Corcoran flexed his knuckles. 'Yeah, it was well out of order, that was.'

'Why don't you crawl back to your maths books, Dimbo?' said Pete Hughes. 'We'll handle this from now on.'

Abby tried to make a break for it, but Animal jumped in

front of her. 'Oi, Brace Face, who's the moron now, eh?'

The others went into a huddle, whispering feverishly until Pete Hughes took control. 'Right,' he said. 'Let's do it.'

Experience had taught me it was pointless to struggle, but it took three of them to drag Abby through the airlock into the bows of the ship.

'Don't touch me, you cretins! You'll regret this; I'll make sure you do!'

The first punishment cell contained a suicidal sailor and his waxwork jailor, but the second was left empty for photo opportunities. They pushed me down onto the cold metal floor. A moment later Abby landed on top of me.

'This is a very bad idea,' said Dimbo. 'The poor girl's practically psychotic. There's no knowing what she might do to him.'

'Button it, brainiac,' said Callum Corcoran, volleying my rucksack through the cell door. 'We're just giving them what they deserve. And if you tell old Catchpole about this, you're a dead Dimbo, OK?'

'Yes but —'

'Think of it as an interesting experiment,' said Pete Hughes. 'The survival of the fattest.'

Callum Corcoran was already chuckling at his own punchline. 'Hey, listen to this. What do you get when you cross a Chickenboy with The Emperor? Ha, ha, ha, ha, ha, ha: Chicken Supreme!'

And they all laughed. All apart from Animal, who was still scratching his head as the cell door slammed shut and the bolt slid slowly across.

1.14 p.m.

Abby's eyes were brimming with pure hatred. Dimbo was right – there was no telling what she might be capable of. And in that tiny cell, there really was nowhere left to hide. It was like that Ultimate Fighting thing Dad had tried to get me interested in. I slid up to the far end of the bare wooden bench, preparing myself for the final assault as she pressed her blood-red fingernails into her palms and formed two tight fists.

I couldn't believe it when she walked straight past me. 'Let me out! Let me out, you morons,' she shrieked, pummelling the door and adding a couple of tornado kicks for good measure. 'I can't stand it in here!'

Her cheeks were covered in angry red blotches and her breathing sounded almost as bad as Granddad's. 'Got to get out, got to get out, got to get out,' she whispered, pacing the three metres from the back of the cell to the door like a deranged lioness.

'Are you all right?' I said.

'What do you care, Chickenboy?'

'You don't sound very well.'

'It's so hot in here,' she said, ripping off her school tie, and then struggling out of her jacket and sweatshirt and dumping them on the floor. 'I can hardly breathe.' She was drenched in sweat. Clumps of damp hair were stuck to the side of her face.

'It doesn't seem that warm to me.'

Abby sank onto the bench and started sobbing. 'I'm suffocating in here.'

And that's when I remembered Mum's recyclable paper bag. 'You're hyperventilating,' I said. 'Here, breathe into this, my mum says it helps.'

I thought she was going to flip when I mentioned Mum, but she took the bag all the same.

After a while her breathing seemed easier.

'Any better?'

She nodded and handed me a pink tissue.

'What's that for?'

'You're bleeding. It's freaking me out.'

If it was so hot in here, why was she shivering? 'What's the matter with you, Abigail?'

'I can't stand small spaces.'

'It's called claustrophobia.'

'I know what it's called, Chickenboy. I just need something to take my mind off it.'

'My mum tells her clients to imagine they're on a tropical beach.'

'I'm not interested in your pathetic mother's pathetic pop psychology. Just give me something to read or I'll go mad in here.'

She was almost as bad as Dimbo – you hardly ever saw her without a book in her hand. 'Didn't you bring something with you?'

Her lips twisted into a sadistic smile. 'I had other plans.'

'Well, I haven't got anything.'

'What's this then?' she said, reaching into my rucksack and pulling out Granddad's story.

I snatched it away from her. 'It's personal, you can't have it.'

'I don't care what it is,' she said, snatching it back again. 'I *need* something to read.'

'Look, please, just give it to me, OK?'

'What's so special about it, anyway? And who are the three stooges in the photograph?'

'One of them's my granddad. It's his war story. Just give it to me, yeah?'

I tried to wrestle it back again, but she clung to it like a dog with a soggy tennis ball. 'What's the big deal? Why don't you want me to read it?'

The truth slipped out before I could censor myself. 'Because I don't want you saying he was a coward. Because I don't want you saying he was just like me.'

Abby was struggling for breath again. '*Please*, I just need to read something. It makes me feel better. I won't say a word, I promise.'

Perhaps I should have made her beg some more, but she sounded so desperate, it seemed like the right thing to do. 'OK you can read it. But just don't say anything, yeah?'

She nodded gratefully, pulled her legs up to her chest, balanced Granddad's story on her knees and started reading.

And I suddenly realised I wasn't scared any more. Whatever hold Abby might have had over me, it was all in the past. At last, I could see her for what she really was. She wasn't The Emperor, she was just another frightened kid.

1.45 p.m.

We must have been in there at least half an hour before an 'anonymous tipster' alerted Mr Catchpole to our whereabouts. He was seething when he opened the cell door and found Abby re-reading Granddad's story for about the sixth time, and yours truly with a face full of Cheesy Wotsits.

'What in the name of God possessed you both?'

Abby looked better already. 'They locked us in, Mr Catchpole.'

'I'm not completely naïve you know,' he said, waving his Tesco bag at us. 'Have you not listened to any of my PSHE lessons? Did neither of you take part in the role-play on teenage pregnancy?'

'It's true,' sniffed Abby. 'We were trapped. All I've been doing is reading his granddad's war story.'

'Yes, well, I'll take your word for it,' said Mr Catchpole, obviously realising how upset she was. 'Now, why don't you tidy yourselves up a bit and then we'd better get a move on. I've got fifty marauding pre-pubescents terrorising the gift shop.'

We followed him back down the ship. Vera Lynn was still warbling about bluebirds and Churchill was repeating his intention of fighting them here, there, and everywhere when I felt a sweaty hand on my shoulder.

'He wasn't a coward.'

'What?'

'Your granddad,' said Abby. 'He wasn't a coward, you moron.'

'What do you mean?'

'Has Mummy never told you about survivor guilt?'

Everyone jeered as we arrived at the top of the gang-plank.

'Survivor what?'

'Survivor guilt,' said Abby, trying to shield herself from the Year Eight paparazzi who were snapping away on their camera phones. 'It's when a person feels guilty about surviving a traumatic event.'

The whoops and catcalls were getting louder.

'Sometimes they blame themselves for not doing enough to help the ones who didn't make it.'

A shower of Red Bull cans landed at our feet.

'Your granddad's friend was dying. What choice did he have? He had to go without him or he would have died himself. But that doesn't make him a coward.'

They all burst into the Wedding March as Mr Catchpole led us down the gangplank like a frazzled father of the bride. They'd torn up their leaflets to make do-it-yourself confetti and it wouldn't be long before the 'wedding photos' went up in our tutor base.

Abby was every inch the blushing bride. She looked so stressed out I actually felt sorry for her. But I could honestly say it was one of the happiest moments of my life. Because whatever happened next, I knew life would never be as bad again. Things were looking up. And I couldn't wait to tell Granddad.

4.05 p.m.

In spite of its downbeat title, 'Old Man Blues' is actually an up-tempo stomp. It was blasting from my iPod as I walked into the Departure Lounge. Arms swinging to Joe Nanton's trombone solo and enjoying what felt like the first real day of summer, it fitted my mood perfectly. I might have looked like I'd been in the wars (Miss Stanley had insisted on presenting me with a certificate to say I'd suffered a head injury), but compared with four hours before, I was on top of the world.

Petal looked really worried when she saw me. She waddled over at top speed and started saying something I couldn't hear. 'It's OK, Petal,' I shouted. 'It's much worse than it looks; nothing to worry about!'

I dodged past her, taking the steps four at a time and charging down the corridor, so anxious to see Granddad that I hardly noticed the gasping granny crouched over her Zimmer frame, or the dismal smell of cabbage.

'Granddad, Granddad, it's me,' I said excitedly, taking out my earphones and barging in without knocking. 'I know what happened and I don't think you're a . . . '

I was secretly hoping he might be feeling better, but I could hardly believe the transformation. The sun was streaming in through the open windows, and Granddad was staring out at a bunch of primary-school kids chucking water bombs at each other. And when he turned to greet me, he looked about thirty years younger – it was amazing.

But why was he wearing a tracksuit? And why hadn't he

got any hair? And why were there tears rolling down his cheeks?

And then I realised who it was. 'Dad, what are *you* doing here?'

I'd never seen him like that before. He wiped his face on his sleeve and stumbled towards me, like a little boy lost. 'I got your messages. Thanks, Sam.'

'What about the race?'

Dad shook his head. 'I didn't realise how bad he was. Otherwise I would have flown back sooner.'

'Where's Granddad?'

The *Countdown* music echoed up from the residents' lounge. Dad put his hand on my shoulder. 'I'm sorry, son.'

'What do you . . . ?' And then I noticed they'd stripped the bed. 'Oh no . . . he hasn't, has he?'

Dad managed to tell me that he was with Granddad when he died, before we both burst into tears and I cursed myself for getting there too late.

After we'd finished crying, Petal brought Dad a cup of tea, I rooted out Granddad's secret store of pineapple chunks and we started putting the rest of his things into black dustbin liners and carrying them out to the car: Nanny's patchwork quilt, the African figures he got from the Ju-Ju man, some musty paperbacks and a whole load of clothes that, if I knew anything about Mum, wouldn't hit the ground until they got to the Oxfam shop.

'So come on, Sam, what happened to your face?'

'Nothing, it was an accident. I've got a certificate.'

Dad peered squeamishly at the shrivelled figures dozing in front of *Neighbours*. 'I hated sending him here, you know, but he would never have coped on his own. I think he understood that in the end. He was a bit confused to begin with, but believe it or not, we actually managed to have a really good chat.'

'What about?'

'He told me he was proud of me,' said Dad, rooting around in his pocket for the car keys. 'I can't think why.'

'What do you mean?'

'He was a proper man, wasn't he?' he said, zapping the central locking. 'Fought in a World War and everything. How could I possibly compete with that?'

I squeezed the last dustbin liner into the back seat. 'I reckon we should think ourselves lucky there haven't *been* any more World Wars.'

'Yes, yes, you're right,' said Dad. 'Come on, we'd better go and check we haven't missed anything.'

'Dad,' I said, reaching under the bed and trying not to sneeze. 'Did you and Granddad talk about anything else?'

Dad was balancing on a footstool, ferreting around in the top of the wardrobe. 'Well, we talked about your nan, how much he both missed her, and . . . you know . . . some other . . . personal things.'

'What sort of things?'

'I don't know,' said Dad, pulling out an old sock, 'this and that.'

I wasn't sure if I should ask, but I really needed to know. 'Did he tell you about Tommy Riley?'

Dad climbed down from the footstool and slumped into Granddad's battered armchair. It was amazing how alike they looked. 'I think he'd tried to tell me before, but it was . . . difficult for him. He was a proud man, Sam. It took a lot of courage.'

'He wasn't a coward, was he, Dad?'

'No, no of course not; he was just a young lad who found himself in an impossible situation.'

I walked over to the window, pretending to be interested in the water fight so that Dad wouldn't see I was crying again. 'I just wish I could have told him. He felt really terrible about it.'

'That's the way it is sometimes. The survivors feel guilty just for surviving.'

'Yes, that's what Abby said.'

'Who's Abby?' said Dad, giving me a toe-curling parental wink. 'Not this mystery girlfriend your mother's been telling me about?'

'Trust me, she's not my girlfriend.'

Dad joined me at the window. 'He was so much calmer after he'd told me. He said he was ready to die.' Dad laid his hand gently on my shoulder. 'There was one thing that was worrying him though.'

'What was that?'

'*You*, Sam. He said you were upset about something. He wasn't sure what it was, but he thought it probably had something to do with school. Was he right?'

I still didn't want to tell him. Even after all I'd been through, it felt as though I'd failed somehow. But if

Granddad could do it, I could too. So I told Dad everything, starting with my cyber-murder and the Chickenboyz website, right through to finding out that one of my persecutors was also my so-called best friend. And after I'd finished, I actually felt a lot better.

I wish I could have said the same for Dad. He looked like he was about to spontaneously combust. 'Why didn't you tell me about this?'

'I knew you'd be angry.'

Dad shook his head in disgust. I really wished I hadn't told him. 'Why should I be angry?'

'Because you warned me about it, didn't you, Dad, about showing my feelings in public? But I turned out to be just like that boy at your school, you know, "the boy who cried"?'

'Oh Sam, I'm so sorry, I should have told you.'

'Told me what?'

'It was *me*,' said Dad. 'I was "the boy who cried". And I hated the idea of the same thing happening to you. We might not have had the internet back then, but they still managed to make my life a misery – some hard man, eh, Sam?'

'Why didn't you tell me?'

'I've never told anyone,' said Dad softly.

'Not even Nanny and Granddad?'

'Of course not. I can see now how stupid it was, but I thought they'd be ashamed of me.'

And then Dad did something he hadn't done for ages. He pulled me towards him and gave me a sweaty cuddle. 'Don't worry, son, we'll sort it out, I promise.'

181

'Thanks, Dad.'

'Right,' he said, taking a last lingering look around Granddad's old room, 'let's get the hell out of here!'

'I'M BEGINNING TO
SEE THE LIGHT'

Petal did a beautiful unaccompanied version of this 1945 Ellington standard at the funeral, which would have pleased Granddad. And I spotted a misplaced apostrophe in the order of service, which would have pleased him even more.

It's been nearly a year now since he died, and I still miss him like crazy. But the funny thing is, every so often, he pops up at my side: whenever I smell burning leaves, ride the underground, swim underwater, watch *The Weakest Link*, eat a Mars Bar or listen to hot jazz, I can feel Granddad enjoying it too. Like he said, 'We share the same genes.' I suppose he'll always be a part of me till my dying day.

And what about school? You probably want me to tell you that things got better straightaway. It was a bit more gradual than that. Mrs Baxter, the head of Year Eight, assured us that St Thomas's Community College took all such incidents very seriously, and Dad, who was almost as nervous as I was, said that in his day the only people with bullying policies were the other kids.

Alex spent an afternoon in the isolation unit, and Abby was excluded for a week. When she came back, they'd made up this stupid song called 'The Emperor's New Clothes' and Pete Hughes kept calling her the Psychotic Penguin, so it was probably a relief when her mum dumped Alex's dad and they went to live in Manchester.

I was given a student mentor and a couple of leaflets about anti-bullying websites, which didn't stop them putting chicken feed in my rucksack or calling me Bernard Matthews, but it still felt much better to have it out in the open. Little by little, they began losing interest. Callum Corcoran even started laughing at my jokes again, until, last term, the chicken noises stopped altogether (apart from Animal of course).

Granddad always said there was nothing worse than a story with a fatuous moral at the end: *'Always believe in yourself, you can do anything if you want it badly enough – that sort of gumph.'* But even if there isn't a moral to my little tale, I'd like to think that at least we've all learned something.

Mum took down the photo of little Harry Potter in her office. She said she'd never forgive herself for failing to spot the classic symptoms of 'the peer persecution scenario', and my best mate, Steve, made a joke about the child psychiatrist's kid always being screwed up. I don't call him Dimbo now – he doesn't like it.

Dad decided he didn't want to be a Hardman any more. He said he was tired of pretending to be something he wasn't. Me and Mum were delighted. But not *quite* so delighted when he told us he was going back to his 'first love'. A few emails later, three out of four of the original band members were reunited and the Kitten Drowners started rehearsing in our garage every other Sunday. It's not what I call music, but they seem to enjoy it, so where's the harm?

And what about me, what have I learned? Well, I'll tell you one thing for a start – if *my* grandchildren ever ask me how I came by the cool, five-centimetre scar on my forehead, I won't tell them it was fighting the forces of evil or masterminding an undercover mission for MI6. I'll tell them I got it running away from a twelve-year-old girl.

Try these other gripping books by Piccadilly Press:

THE LONDON MURDER MYSTERIES

The MONTGOMERY MURDER

CORA HARRISON

In the mean streets of Victorian London lies the body of
wealthy Mr Montgomery. The police need an insider,
someone streetwise, cunning, bold . . . someone like Alfie.
When Inspector Denham makes him an offer he can't
refuse, it's up to Alfie and his gang to sift clues, shadow
suspects and negotiate a sinister world of double-dealing
and danger – until the shocking truth is revealed.

HATTORI HACHI

The Revenge of Praying Mantis

JANE PROWSE

Hattie Jackson is just an ordinary fifteen-year-old – until
her mother disappears and Hattie's life is turned upside
down. With the help of her friend Mad Dog,
Hattie discovers the truth about her mother's 'other life'
and the role she must now take on to defeat a terrifying
league of evil ninjutsu warriors, led by Praying Mantis –
the most deadly assassin known to man . . .

THE SPELLBOUND HOTEL

TOM EGLINGTON

Strange things are happening in the village of
Stagtree Knoll, to everyone except Bethany.
Determined to find out what's going on, she sneaks
into the mysterious Stoames Mansion and discovers a
hotel for ghosts, spirits and non-material beings.
But Bethany is not a welcome guest here and if she
hopes to escape and save the village, she must face
the sinister power at the heart of the hotel, and break
the spell it has cast over everyone.

Desperate Measures

LAURA SUMMERS

Vicky and Rhianna are twins but they couldn't be more
different. For their fourteenth birthday, Vicky wants a
card from the hottest boy in school. Rhianna,
brain-damaged at birth, wants a Furby.
Instead, they get a nasty shock – their foster parents can't
cope and it looks as if Vicky and Rhianna and their
younger brother Jamie will have to be split up.
How can they stay together?
Desperate times call for desperate measures . . .

☆

www.piccadillypress.co.uk

☆ The latest news on forthcoming books

☆ Chapter previews

☆ Author biographies

☆ Fun quizzes

☆ Reader reviews

☆ Competitions and fab prizes

☆ Book features and cool downloads

☆ And much, much more . . .

Log on and check it out!

Piccadilly Press

☆